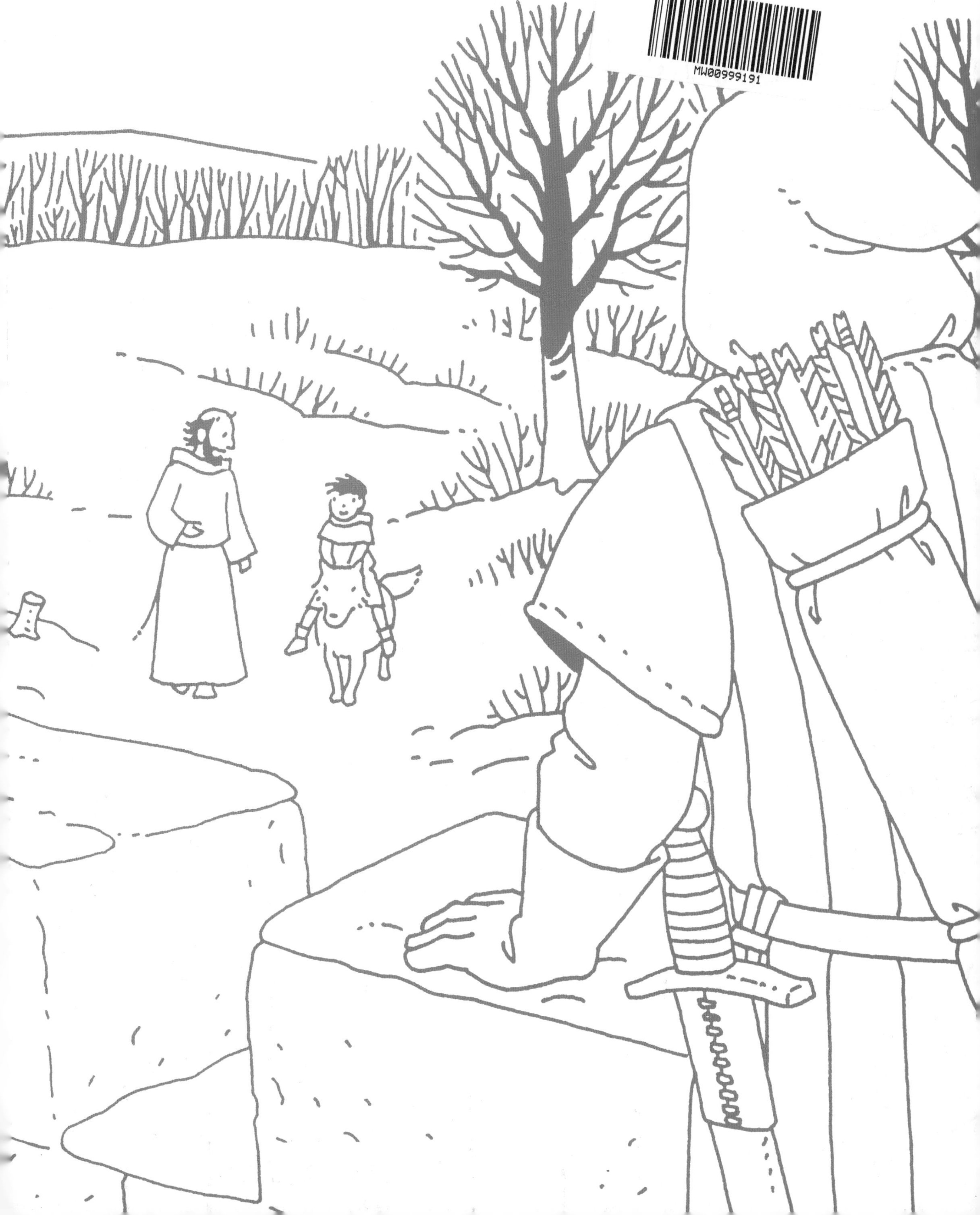

Jean-François Kieffer

The Adventures of LOUPIO

Translated by Carrie Akoun

VOLUME 2

The Hunters
and other stories

MAGNIFICAT • Ignatius

Original French edition: *Les Aventures de Loupio*
Tome 2: Les Chasseurs et autres récits
© 2002 by Fleurus-Edifa, Paris
© 2011 by Ignatius Press, San Francisco • Magnificat, New-york
All rights reserved
ISBN Ignatius Press 978-1-58617-624-2
ISBN Magnificat 978-1-936260-16-4

Printed in PRC in May 2022. Job Number MGN 22026
Printed in compliance with the Consumer Protection Safety Act, 2008.

Table of Contents

FRANCIS OF ASSISI

lived a poor but joyful life during
the era of knights and troubadours. Son of
a rich merchant of the city of Assisi in Italy,
this young man decided to give up his fortune
and his dreams of glory so as to serve God
better. Free from material goods, he became
a brother and a friend to all living creatures.
It is said that Francis spoke to birds and
that one day he changed a wolf's heart.
Some even say that this wolf befriended
an orphan child and that the two of them
roamed the roads of Italy, having
a thousand adventures …

The Hunters

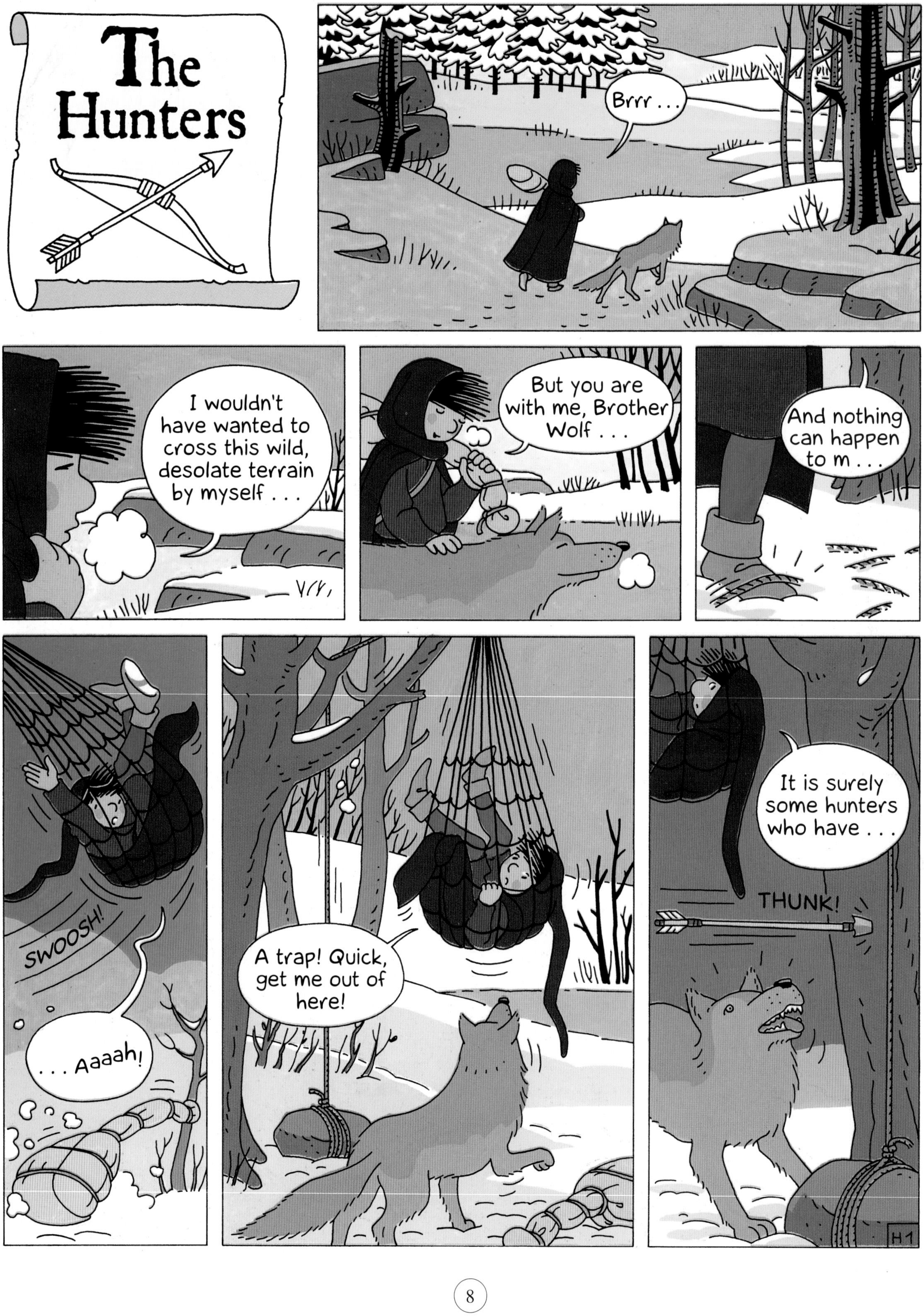
Brrr . . .
I wouldn't have wanted to cross this wild, desolate terrain by myself . . .
But you are with me, Brother Wolf . . .
And nothing can happen to m . . .
SWOOSH!
. . . Aaaah!
A trap! Quick, get me out of here!
It is surely some hunters who have . . .
THUNK!

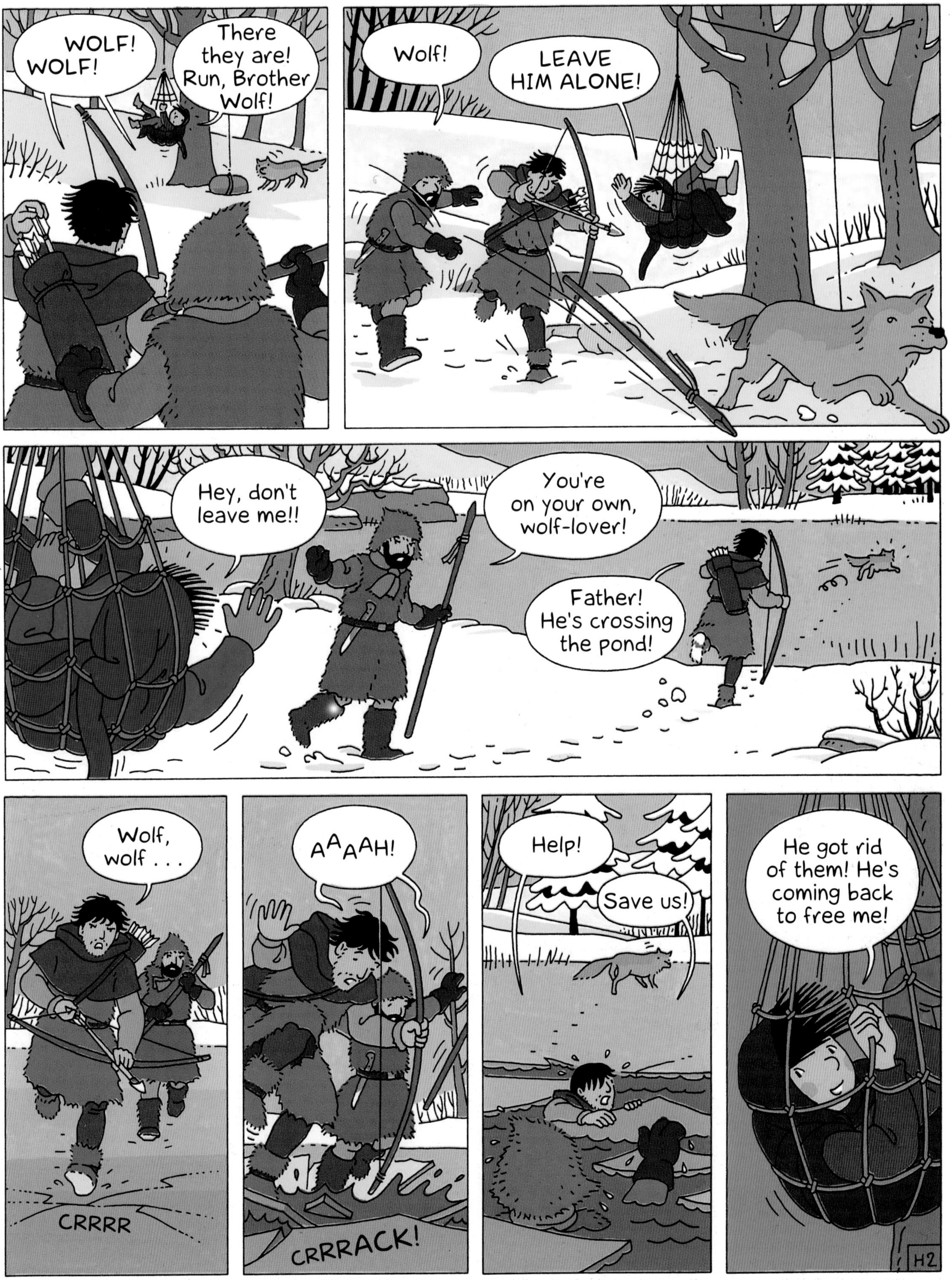
WOLF! WOLF!
There they are! Run, Brother Wolf!
Wolf!
LEAVE HIM ALONE!
Hey, don't leave me!!
You're on your own, wolf-lover!
Father! He's crossing the pond!
Wolf, wolf . . .
CRRRR
AAAAH!
CRRRACK!
Help!
Save us!
He got rid of them! He's coming back to free me!
H2

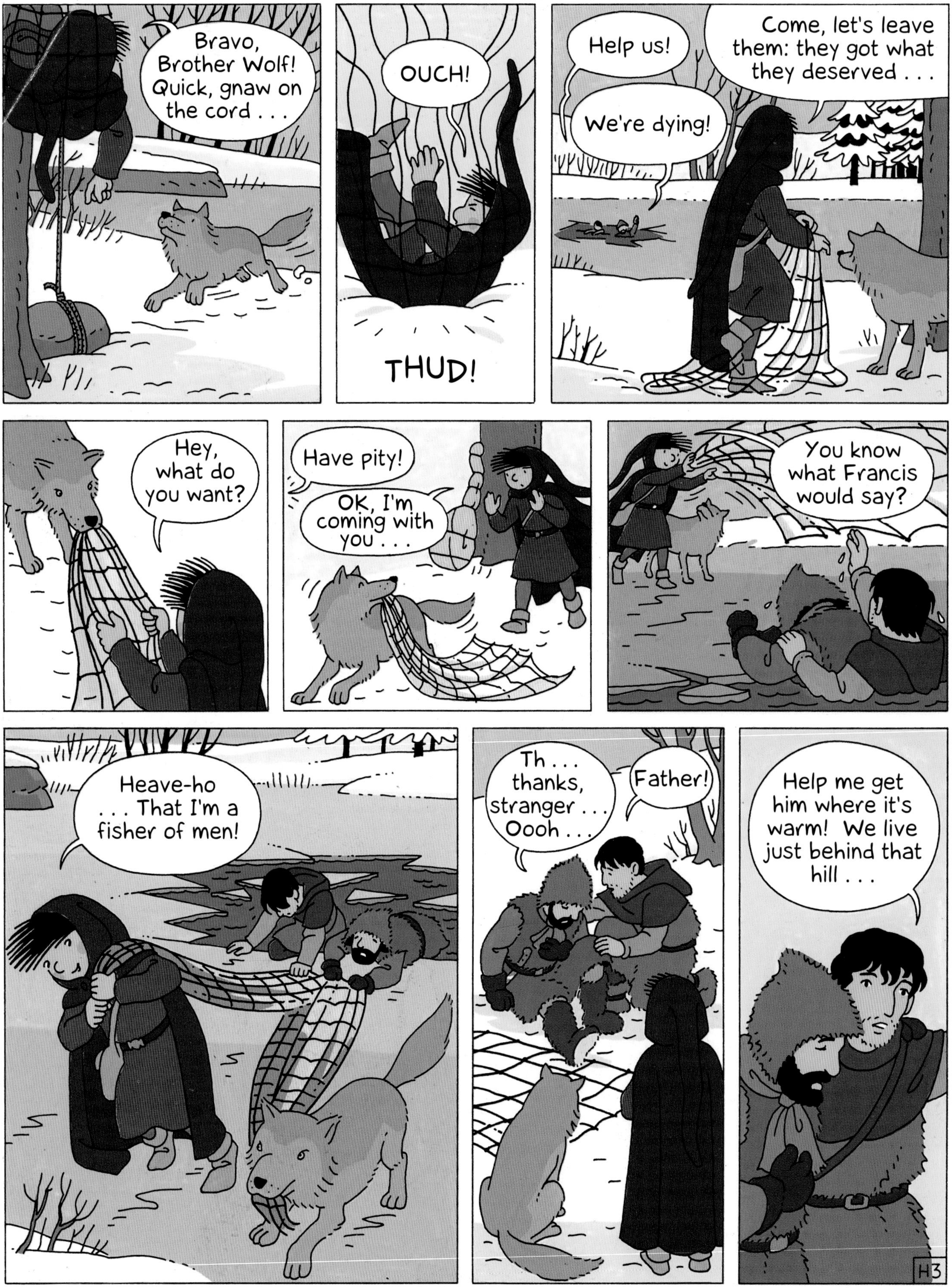
Bravo, Brother Wolf! Quick, gnaw on the cord . . .
OUCH!
THUD!
Help us!
We're dying!
Come, let's leave them: they got what they deserved . . .
Hey, what do you want?
Have pity!
OK, I'm coming with you . . .
You know what Francis would say?
Heave-ho . . . That I'm a fisher of men!
Th . . . thanks, stranger . . . Oooh . . .
Father!
Help me get him where it's warm! We live just behind that hill . . .
H3

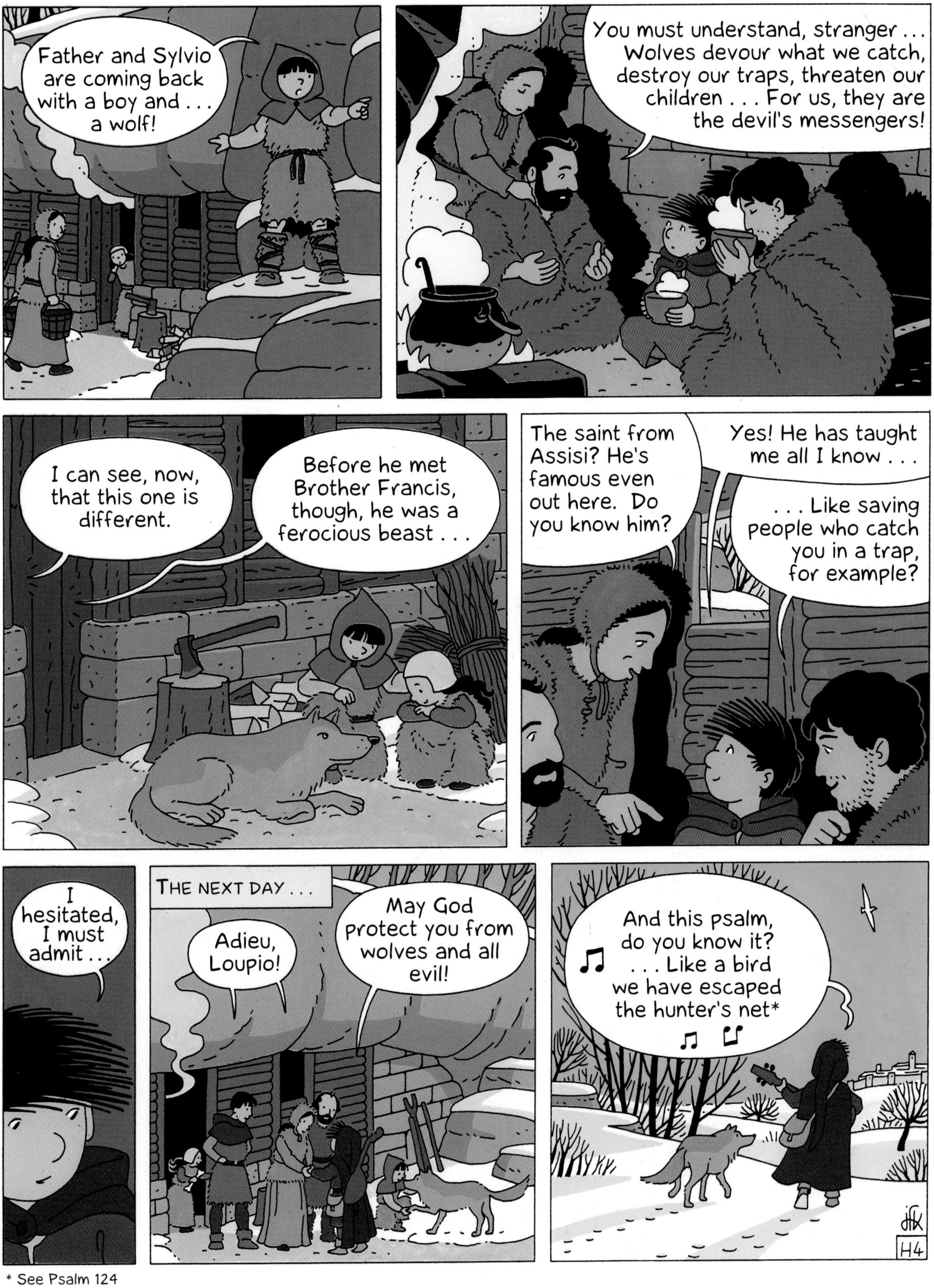
Father and Sylvio are coming back with a boy and . . . a wolf!
You must understand, stranger . . . Wolves devour what we catch, destroy our traps, threaten our children . . . For us, they are the devil's messengers!
I can see, now, that this one is different.
Before he met Brother Francis, though, he was a ferocious beast . . .
The saint from Assisi? He's famous even out here. Do you know him?
Yes! He has taught me all I know . . .
. . . Like saving people who catch you in a trap, for example?
I hesitated, I must admit . . .
THE NEXT DAY . . .
Adieu, Loupio!
May God protect you from wolves and all evil!
And this psalm, do you know it? . . . Like a bird we have escaped the hunter's net*
H4

* See Psalm 124

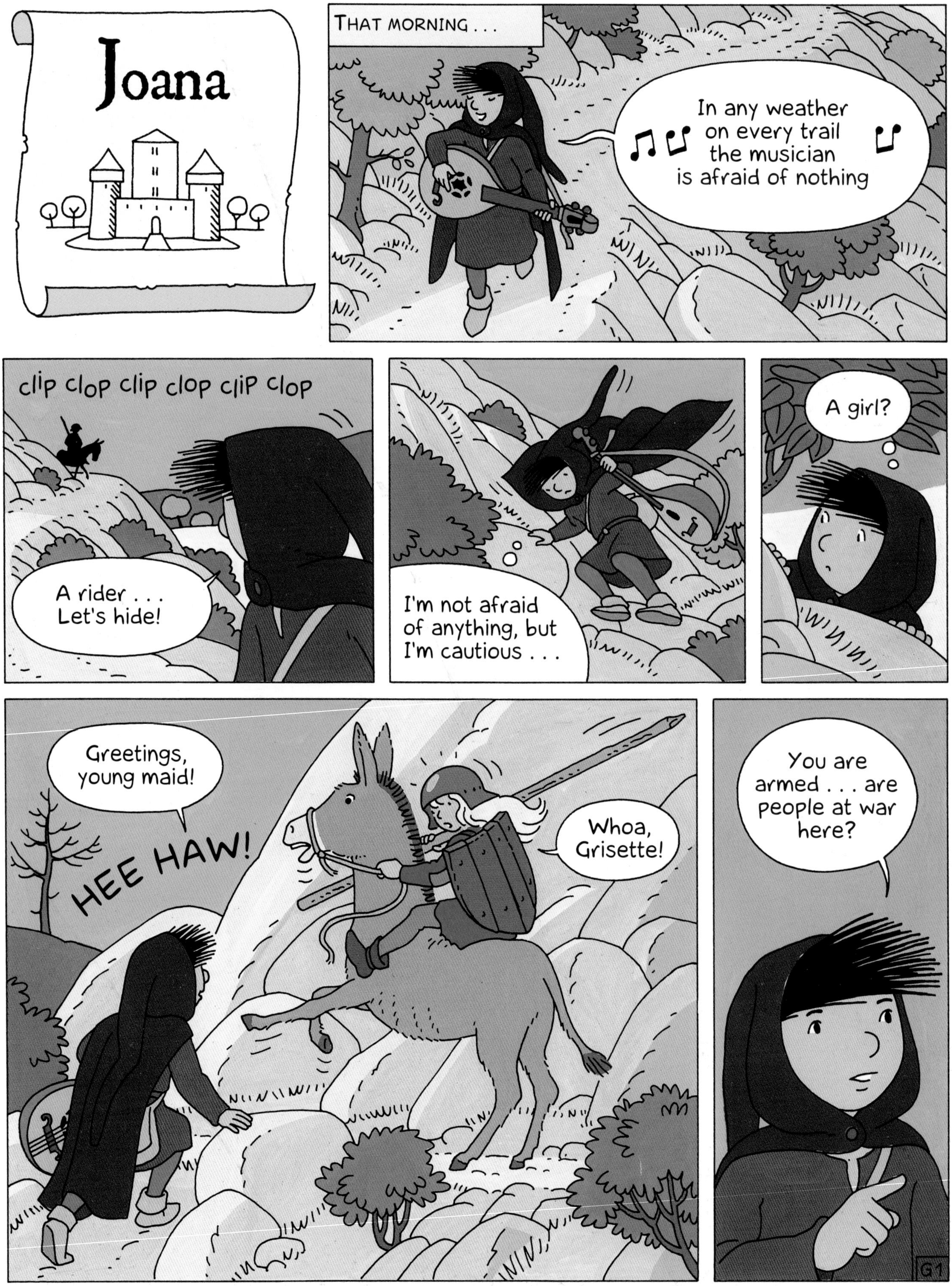
Joana
THAT MORNING . . .
In any weather on every trail the musician is afraid of nothing
clip clop clip clop clip clop
A rider . . . Let's hide!
I'm not afraid of anything, but I'm cautious . . .
A girl?
Greetings, young maid!
HEE HAW!
Whoa, Grisette!
You are armed . . . are people at war here?
G1

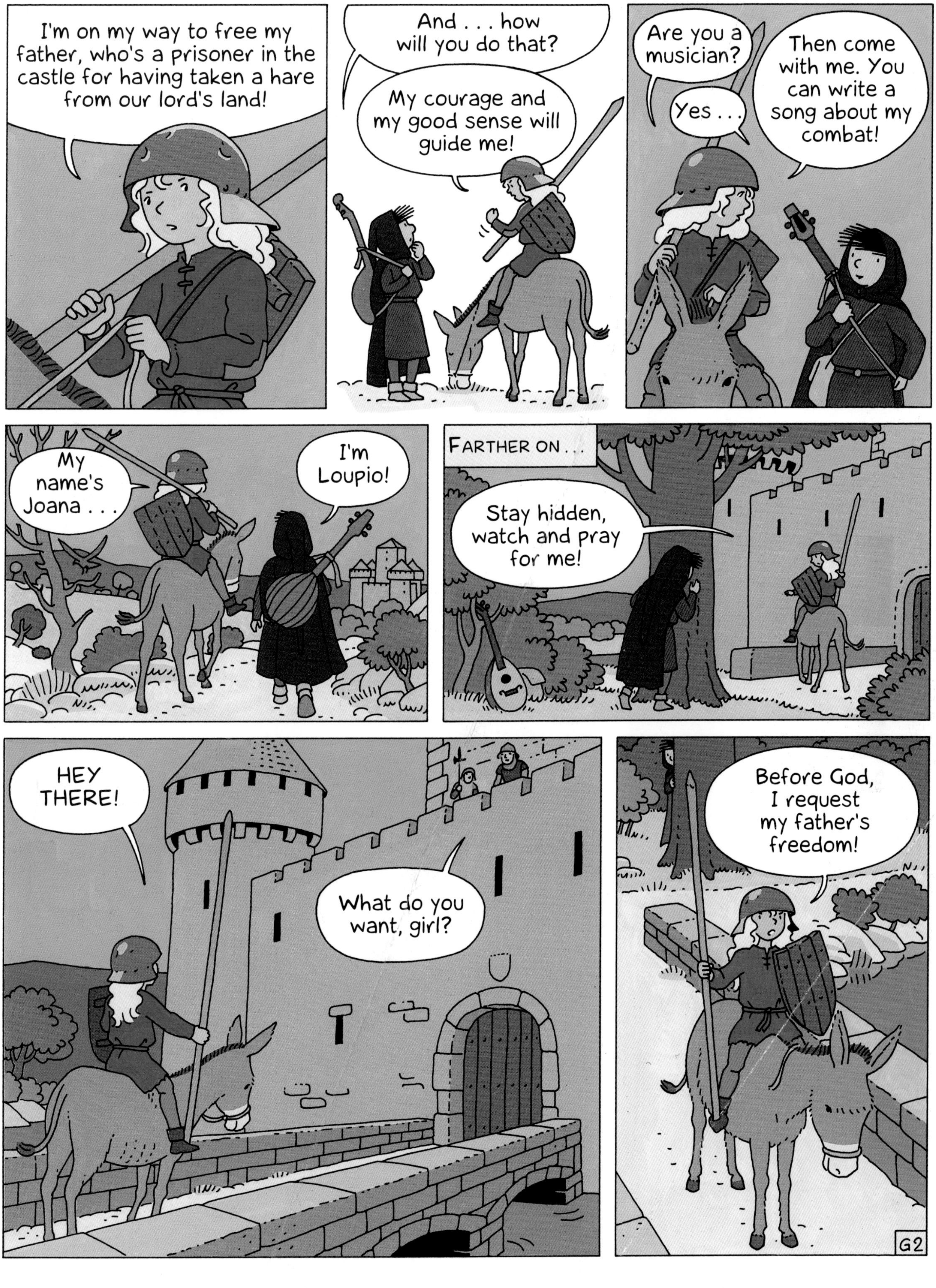
I'm on my way to free my father, who's a prisoner in the castle for having taken a hare from our lord's land!
And . . . how will you do that?
My courage and my good sense will guide me!
Are you a musician?
Yes . . .
Then come with me. You can write a song about my combat!
My name's Joana . . .
I'm Loupio!
FARTHER ON . . .
Stay hidden, watch and pray for me!
HEY THERE!
What do you want, girl?
Before God, I request my father's freedom!
G2

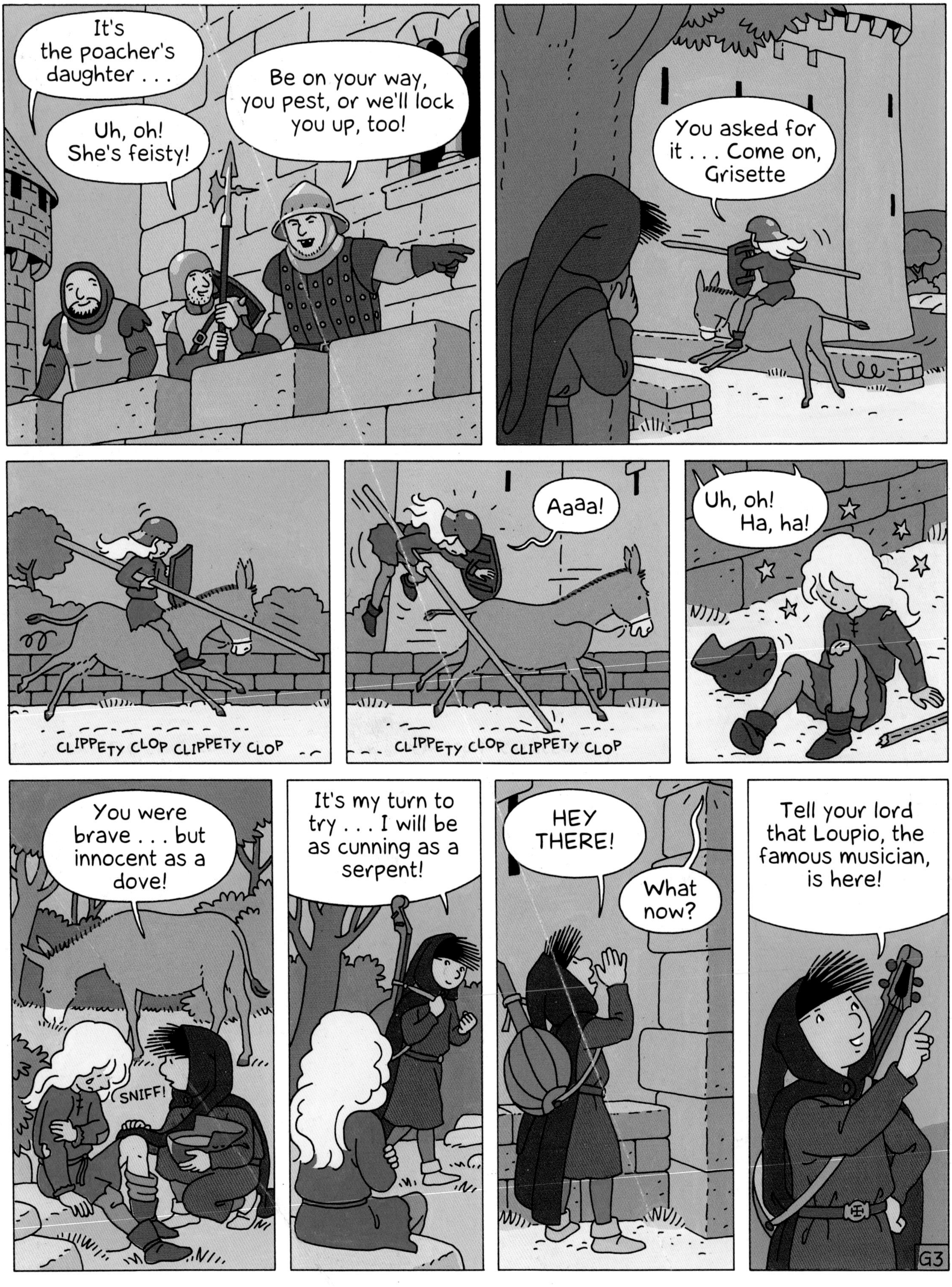
It's the poacher's daughter . . .
Uh, oh! She's feisty!
Be on your way, you pest, or we'll lock you up, too!
You asked for it . . . Come on, Grisette
CLIPPETY CLOP CLIPPETY CLOP
Aaaa!
CLIPPETY CLOP CLIPPETY CLOP
Uh, oh! Ha, ha!
You were brave . . . but innocent as a dove!
SNIFF!
It's my turn to try . . . I will be as cunning as a serpent!
HEY THERE!
What now?
Tell your lord that Loupio, the famous musician, is here!
G3

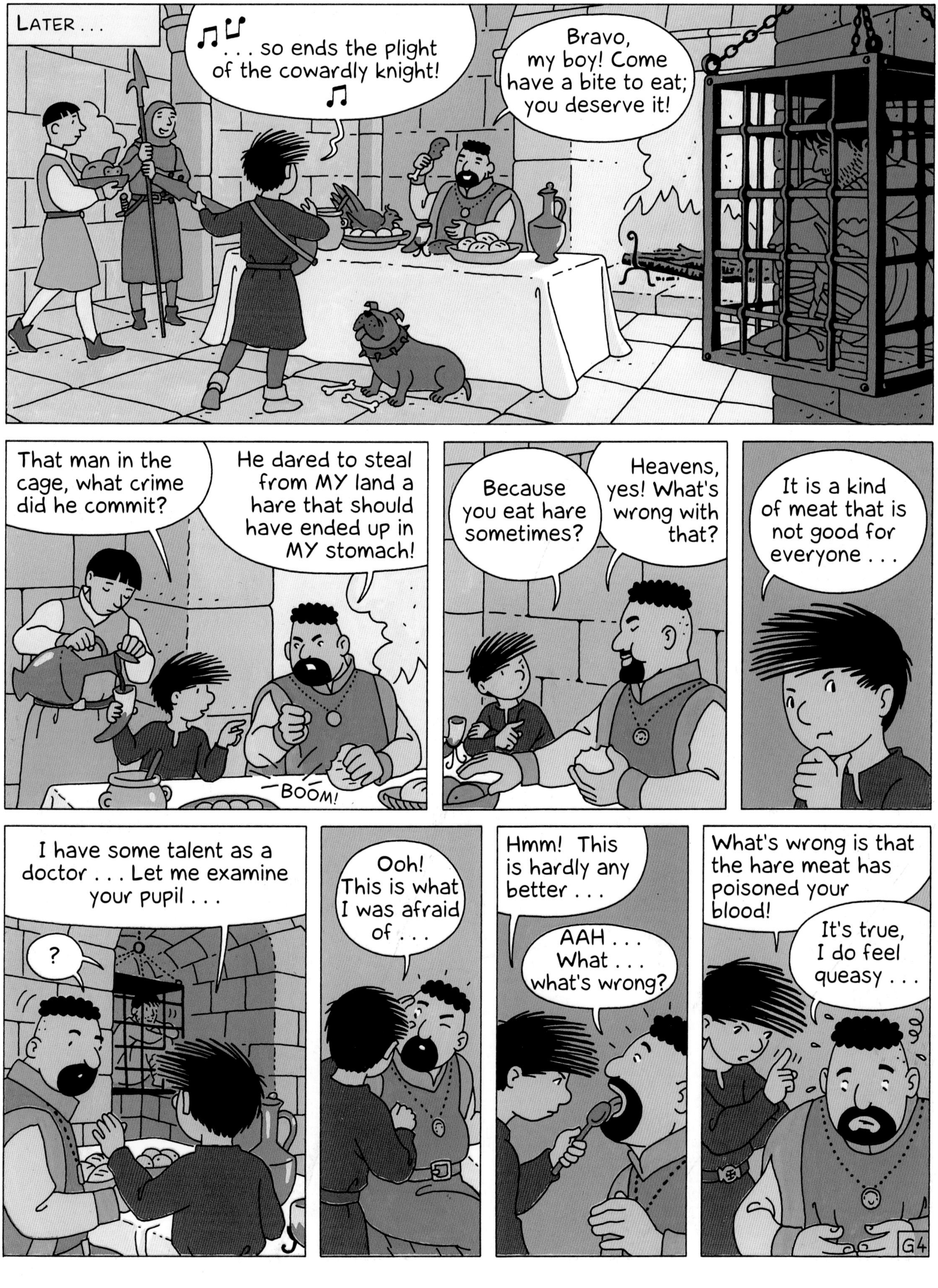

LATER . . .
. . . so ends the plight of the cowardly knight!
Bravo, my boy! Come have a bite to eat; you deserve it!
That man in the cage, what crime did he commit?
He dared to steal from MY land a hare that should have ended up in MY stomach!
BOOM!
Because you eat hare sometimes?
Heavens, yes! What's wrong with that?
It is a kind of meat that is not good for everyone . . .
I have some talent as a doctor . . . Let me examine your pupil . . .
?
Ooh! This is what I was afraid of . . .
Hmm! This is hardly any better . . .
AAH . . . What . . . what's wrong?
What's wrong is that the hare meat has poisoned your blood!
It's true, I do feel queasy . . .
G4

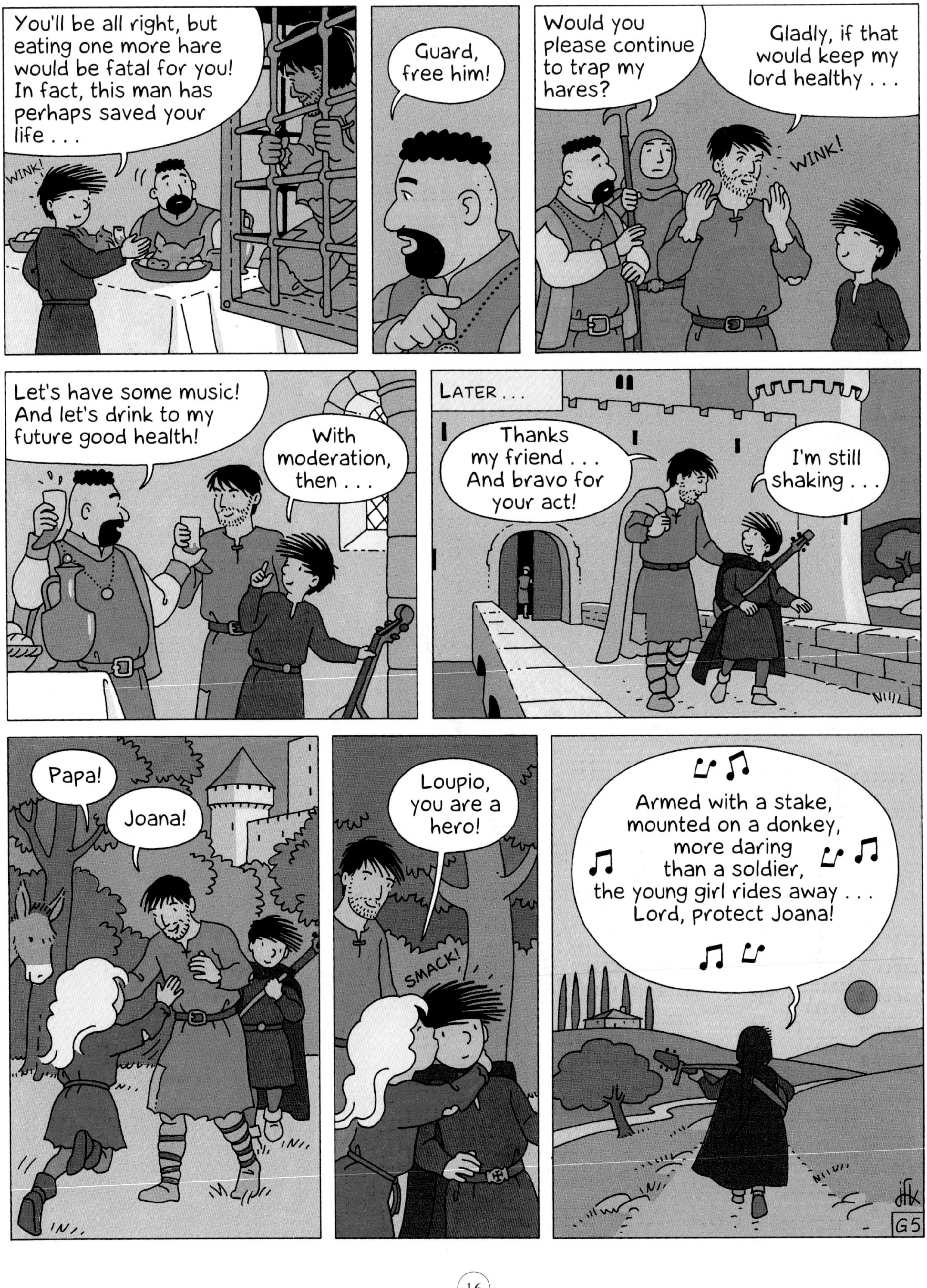
You'll be all right, but eating one more hare would be fatal for you! In fact, this man has perhaps saved your life . . .
WINK!
Guard, free him!
Would you please continue to trap my hares?
Gladly, if that would keep my lord healthy . . .
WINK!
Let's have some music! And let's drink to my future good health!
With moderation, then . . .
LATER . . .
Thanks my friend . . . And bravo for your act!
I'm still shaking . . .
Papa!
Joana!
Loupio, you are a hero!
SMACK!
Armed with a stake, mounted on a donkey, more daring than a soldier, the young girl rides away . . . Lord, protect Joana!
G5

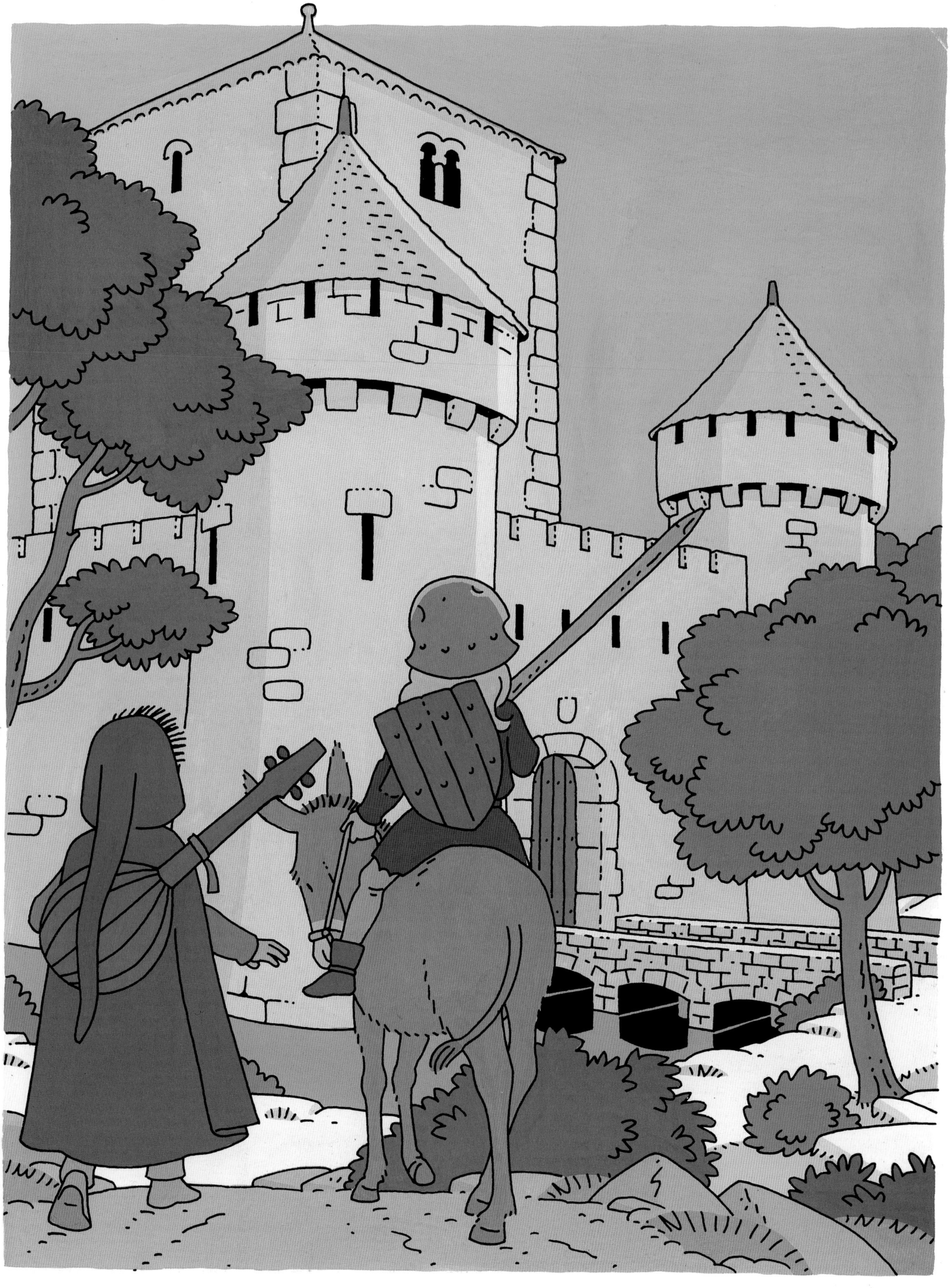

The Three Pearls

Yoo hoo! It's us!

Loupio, Brother Wolf . . . Praise God!

Francis! What is it?

For three days now, I haven't been able to see . . .

We must take care of you! I'll run get old Matteo.

I have never treated this problem . . . But one of my books of potions has a description and a remedy.

Loupio, I could use your precious help . . .

You, Francis, must wait patiently for a few more days. Stay out of the wind and away from light. My wife will bring you hot food and herbal tea.

Stay with him, Brother Wolf . . .

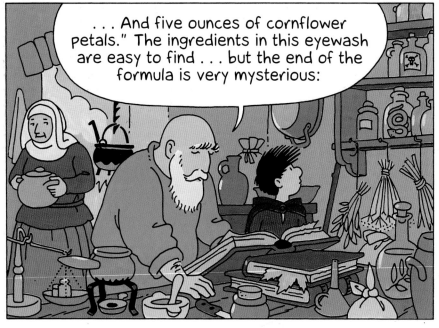

. . . And five ounces of cornflower petals." The ingredients in this eyewash are easy to find . . . but the end of the formula is very mysterious:

"To make the potion boil, into it you must plunge Three Daylight Stars, Three Goosehunter Chips, Three Pearls of Love."

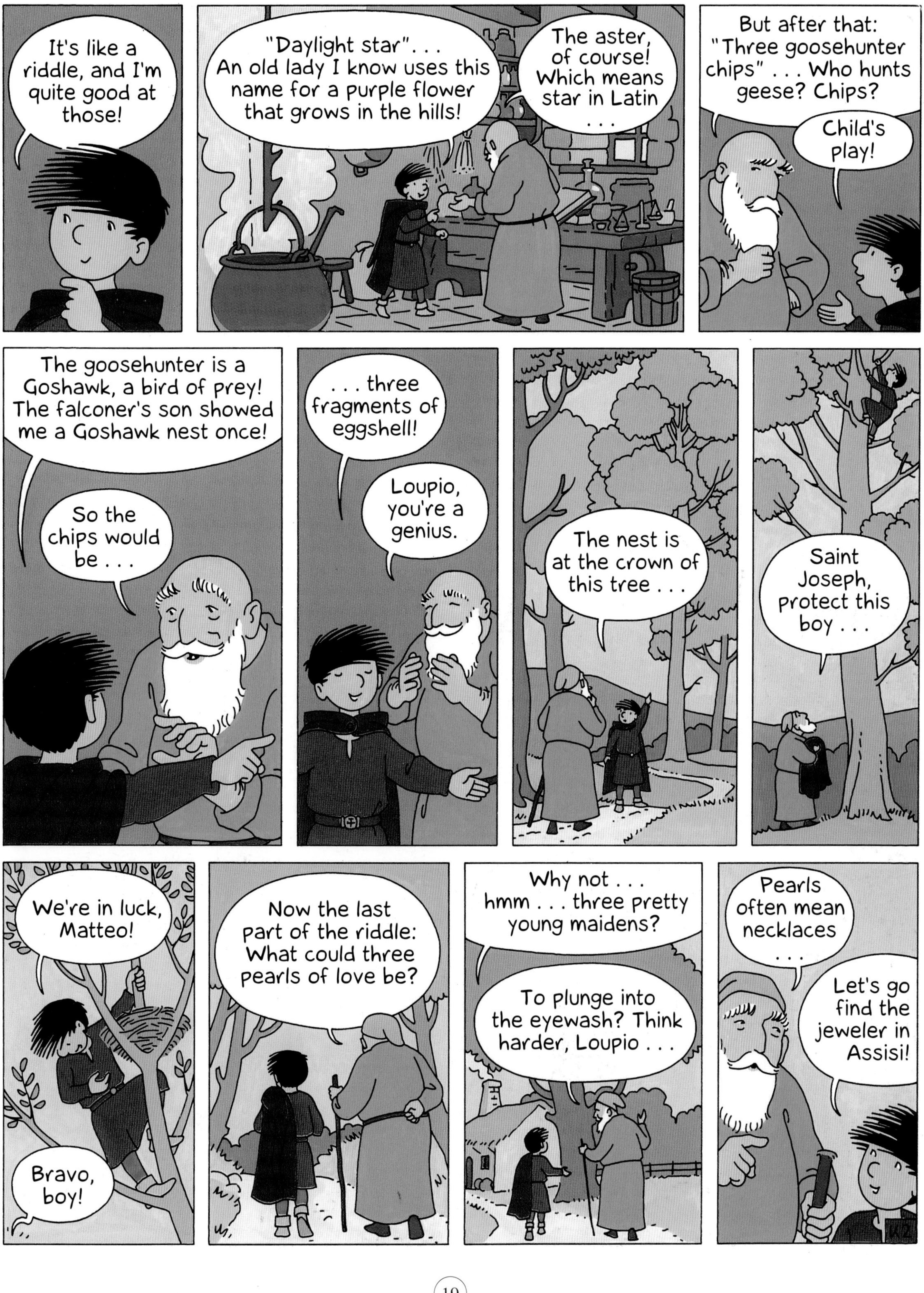
It's like a riddle, and I'm quite good at those!
"Daylight star" . . . An old lady I know uses this name for a purple flower that grows in the hills!
The aster, of course! Which means star in Latin . . .
But after that: "Three goosehunter chips" . . . Who hunts geese? Chips?
Child's play!
The goosehunter is a Goshawk, a bird of prey! The falconer's son showed me a Goshawk nest once!
So the chips would be . . .
. . . three fragments of eggshell!
Loupio, you're a genius.
The nest is at the crown of this tree . . .
Saint Joseph, protect this boy . . .
We're in luck, Matteo!
Bravo, boy!
Now the last part of the riddle: What could three pearls of love be?
Why not . . . hmm . . . three pretty young maidens?
To plunge into the eyewash? Think harder, Loupio . . .
Pearls often mean necklaces . . .
Let's go find the jeweler in Assisi!

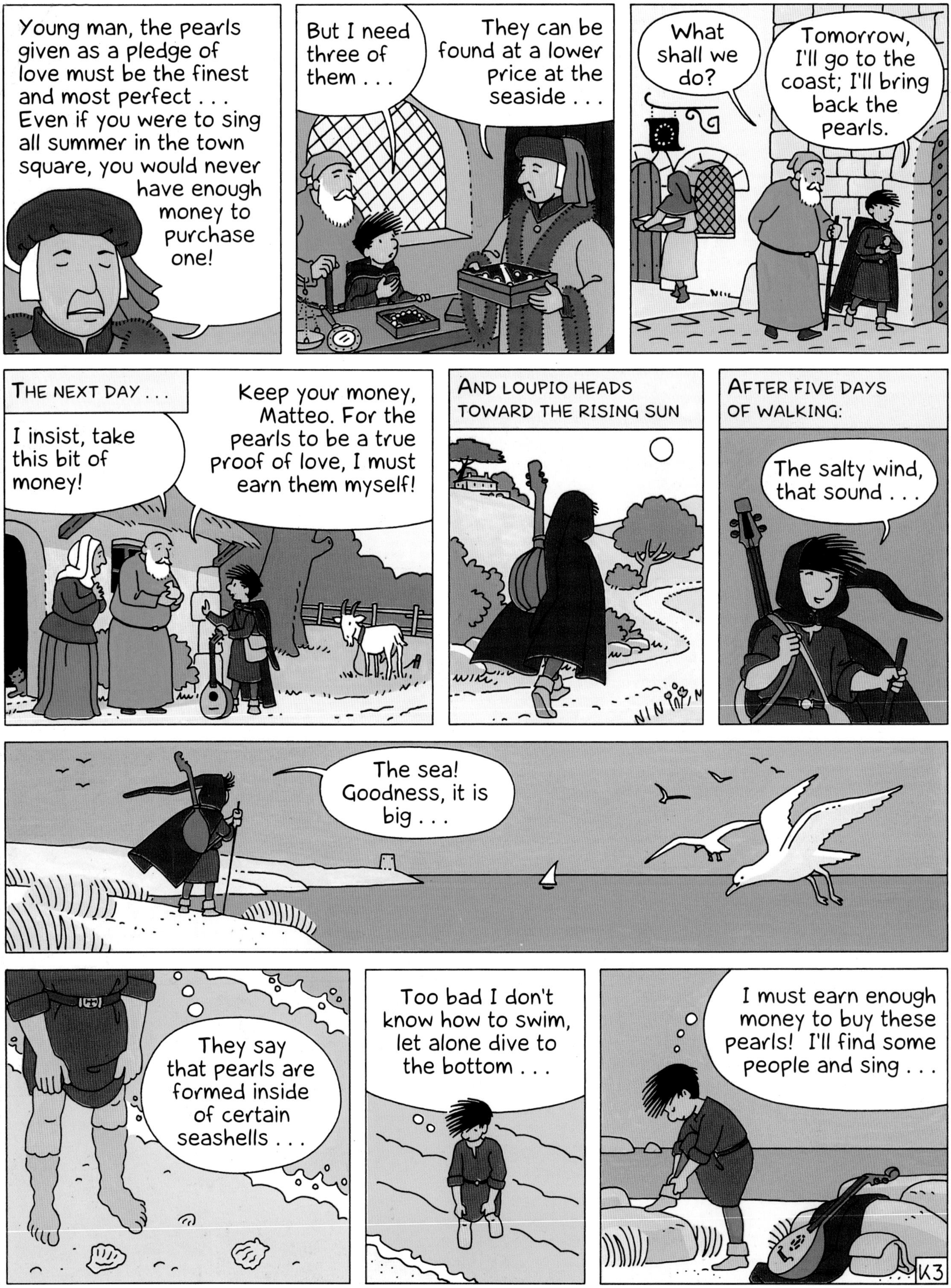
Young man, the pearls given as a pledge of love must be the finest and most perfect . . . Even if you were to sing all summer in the town square, you would never have enough money to purchase one!
But I need three of them . . .
They can be found at a lower price at the seaside . . .
What shall we do?
Tomorrow, I'll go to the coast; I'll bring back the pearls.
THE NEXT DAY . . .
I insist, take this bit of money!
Keep your money, Matteo. For the pearls to be a true proof of love, I must earn them myself!
AND LOUPIO HEADS TOWARD THE RISING SUN
AFTER FIVE DAYS OF WALKING:
The salty wind, that sound . . .
The sea! Goodness, it is big . . .
They say that pearls are formed inside of certain seashells . . .
Too bad I don't know how to swim, let alone dive to the bottom . . .
I must earn enough money to buy these pearls! I'll find some people and sing . . .
K3

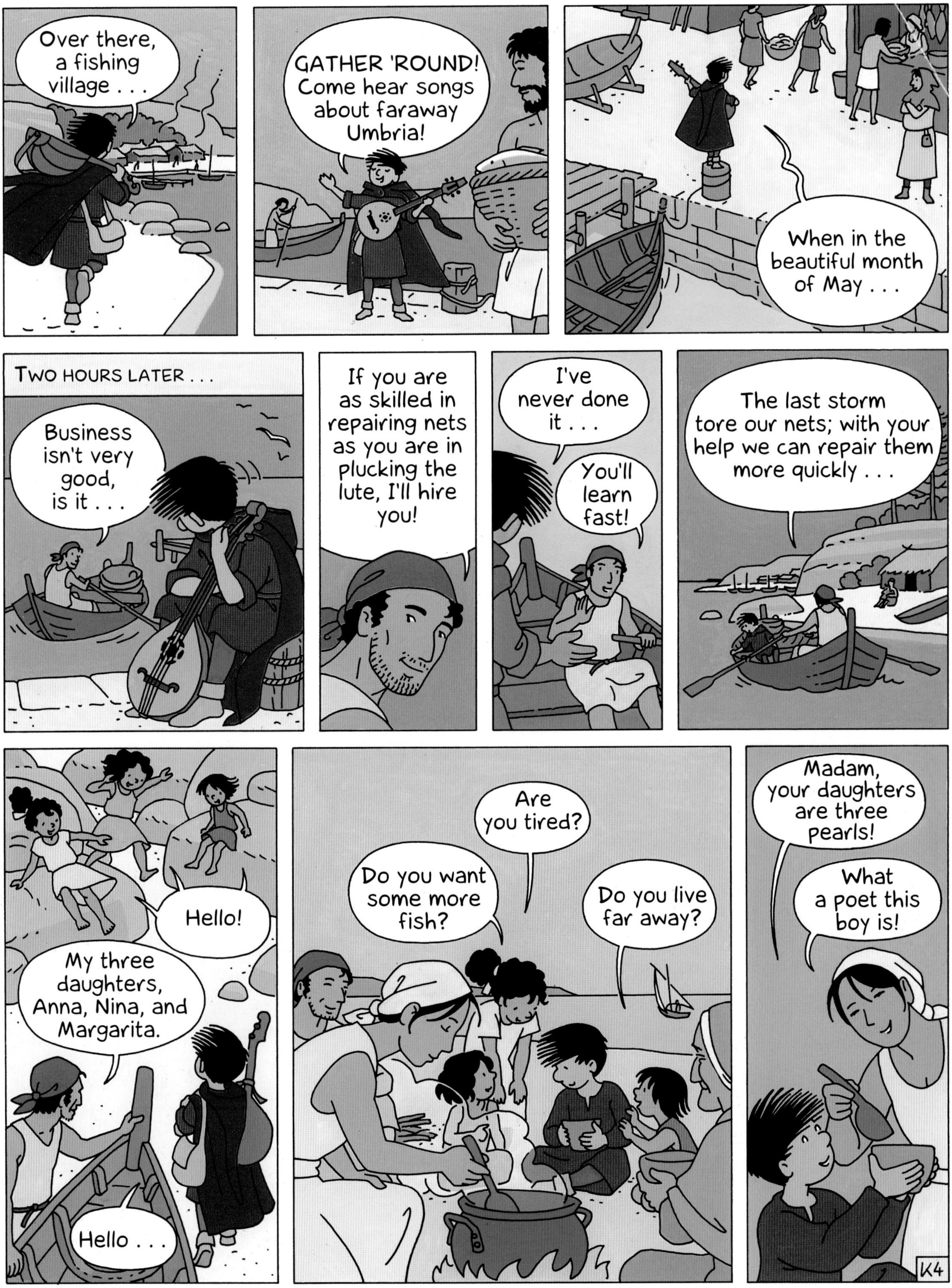

Over there, a fishing village . . .
GATHER 'ROUND! Come hear songs about faraway Umbria!
When in the beautiful month of May . . .
TWO HOURS LATER . . .
Business isn't very good, is it . . .
If you are as skilled in repairing nets as you are in plucking the lute, I'll hire you!
I've never done it . . .
You'll learn fast!
The last storm tore our nets; with your help we can repair them more quickly . . .
Hello!
My three daughters, Anna, Nina, and Margarita.
Hello . . .
Are you tired?
Do you want some more fish?
Do you live far away?
Madam, your daughters are three pearls!
What a poet this boy is!
K4

Hi Hi Hiiiii

Uh, where am I?

Ah, yes: the sea, the fisherman's family . . .

Hi Hiiiii

Sleep well, Loupio?

So, let's get to work before the sun gets too hot!

FOR LOUPIO, IT IS A DAY FULL OF DISCOVERIES . . .

Make it tighter

What heat!

Let's take a little rest . . .

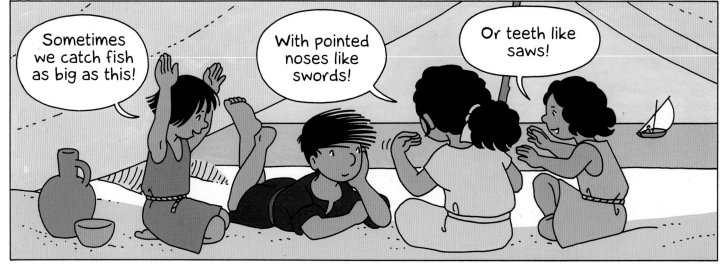

Sometimes we catch fish as big as this!

With pointed noses like swords!

Or teeth like saws!

Oh, you're kidding me!

Not at all!

One day, I got caught in a net myself . . .

Ha, ha!

Let's get back to work.

Ow, my fingers . . .

Could they still play music for us?

I think so!

♫ Like ♪ the sailboat on the sea ♫

It's beautiful!

Bravo!

Now, tell us about . . .

I will tell you about my friend Francis.

This is why I'm here on the coast; to look for pearls . . .

Alas, even at the port of Ancona, they are worth a fortune!

Much more than we could ever give you for your work . . .

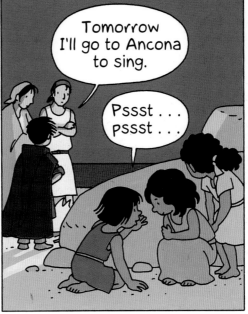

Tomorrow I'll go to Ancona to sing.

Pssst . . . pssst . . .

Follow us, Loupio!

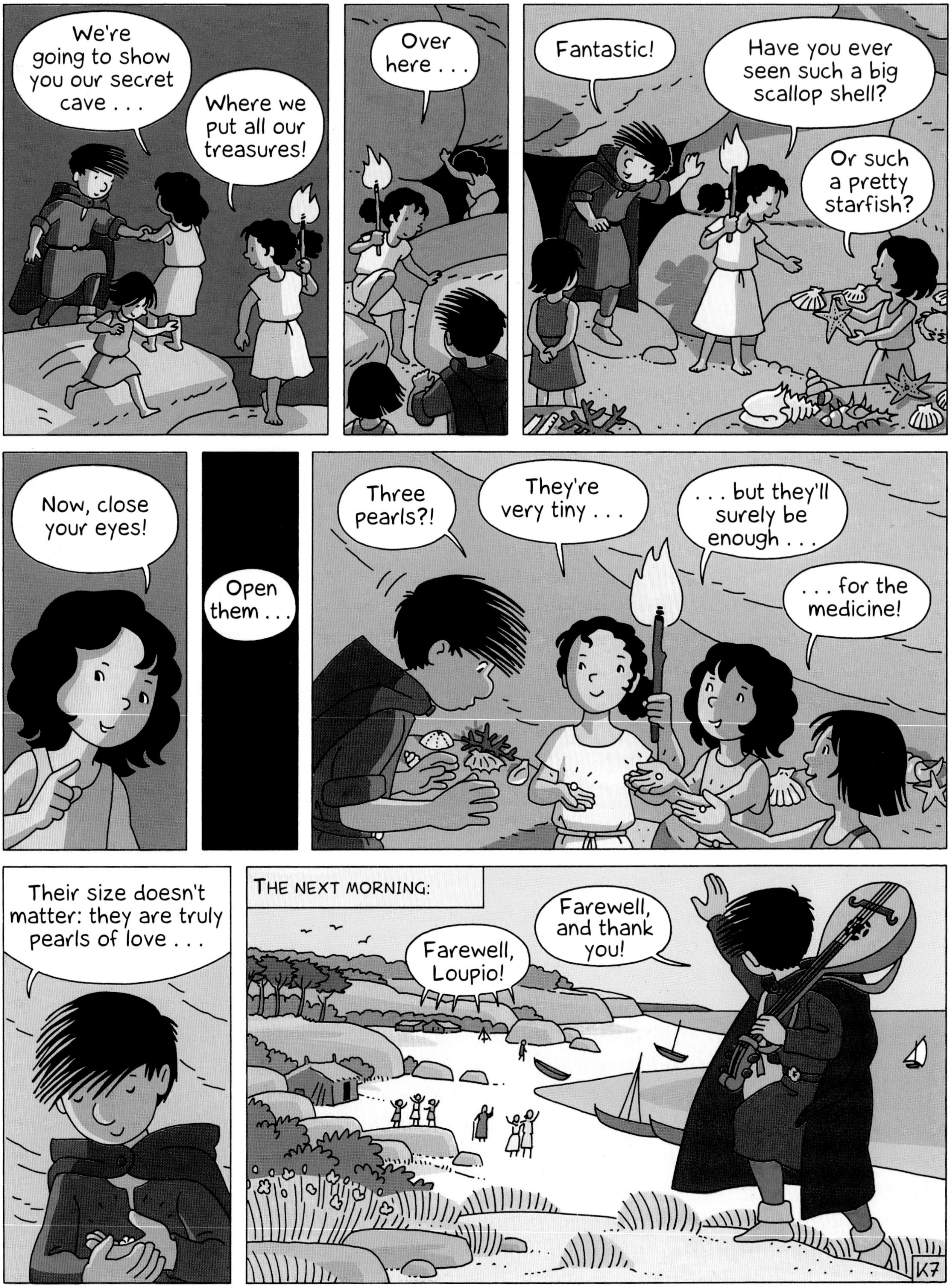

We're going to show you our secret cave . . .
Where we put all our treasures!
Over here . . .
Fantastic!
Have you ever seen such a big scallop shell?
Or such a pretty starfish?
Now, close your eyes!
Open them . . .
Three pearls?!
They're very tiny . . .
. . . but they'll surely be enough . . .
. . . for the medicine!
Their size doesn't matter: they are truly pearls of love . . .
THE NEXT MORNING:
Farewell, Loupio!
Farewell, and thank you!
K7

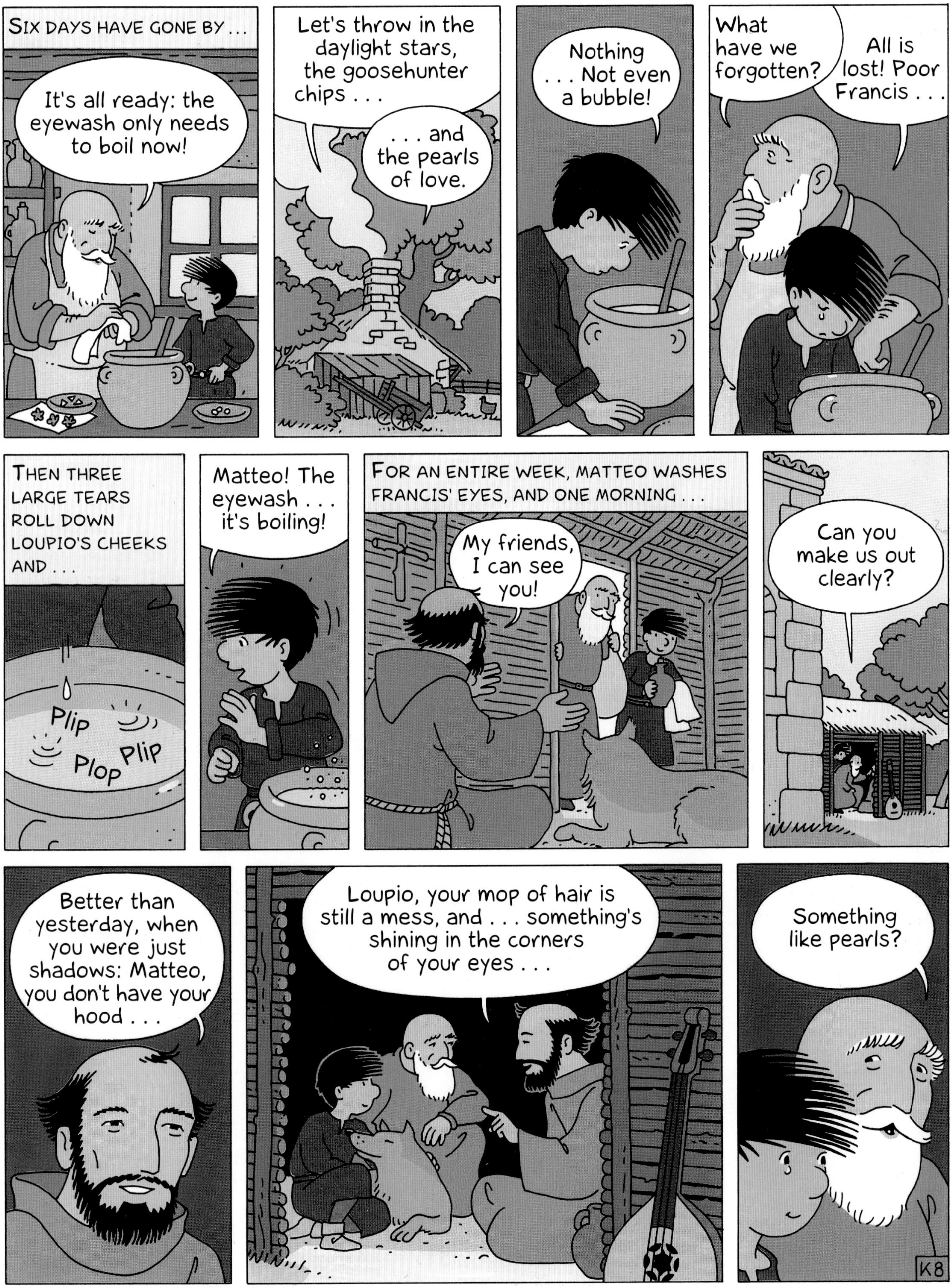
SIX DAYS HAVE GONE BY . . .
It's all ready: the eyewash only needs to boil now!
Let's throw in the daylight stars, the goosehunter chips . . .
. . . and the pearls of love.
Nothing . . . Not even a bubble!
What have we forgotten?
All is lost! Poor Francis . . .
THEN THREE LARGE TEARS ROLL DOWN LOUPIO'S CHEEKS AND . . .
Plip
Plop
Plip
Matteo! The eyewash . . . it's boiling!
FOR AN ENTIRE WEEK, MATTEO WASHES FRANCIS' EYES, AND ONE MORNING . . .
My friends, I can see you!
Can you make us out clearly?
Better than yesterday, when you were just shadows: Matteo, you don't have your hood . . .
Loupio, your mop of hair is still a mess, and . . . something's shining in the corners of your eyes . . .
Something like pearls?
K8

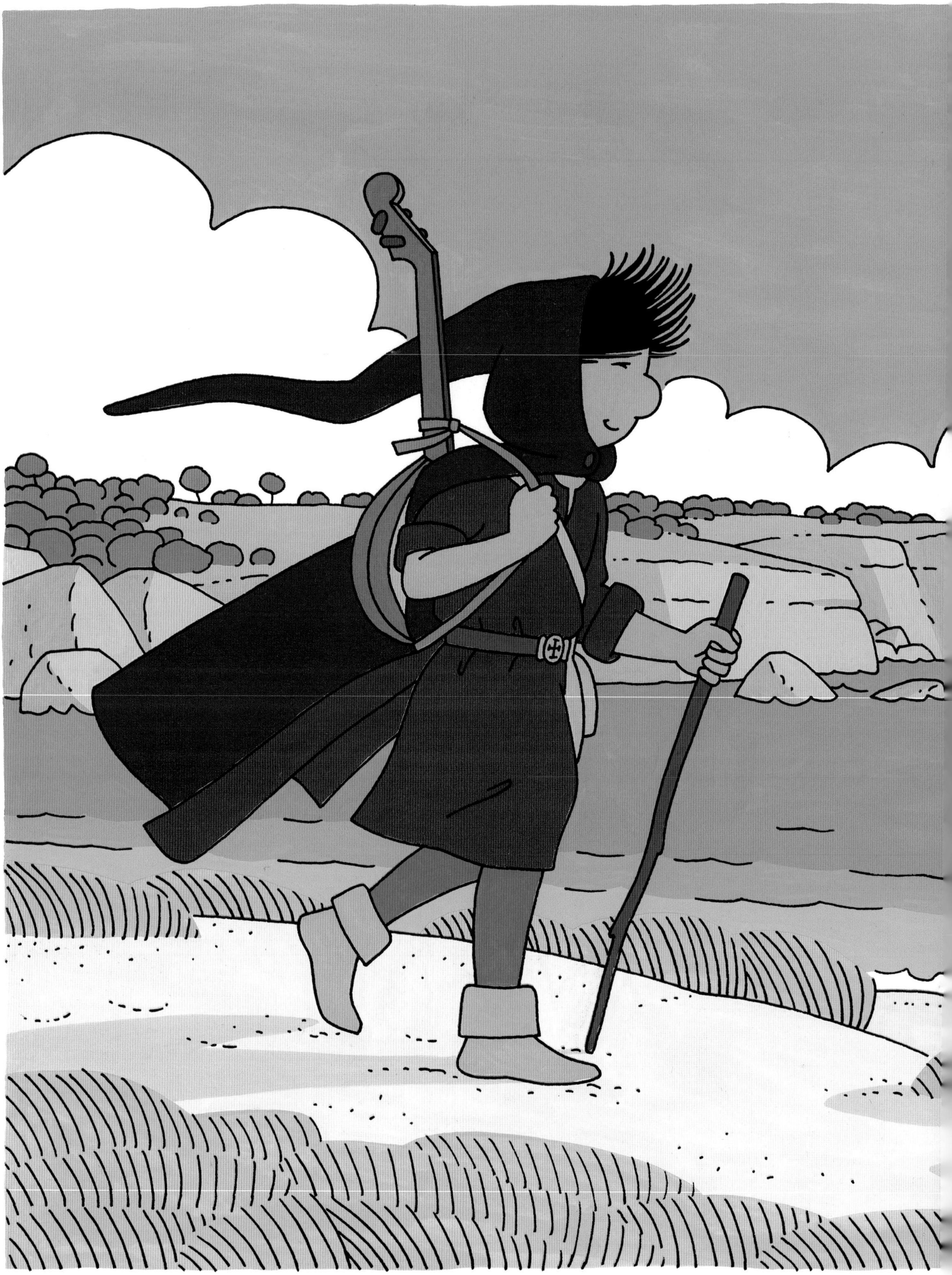

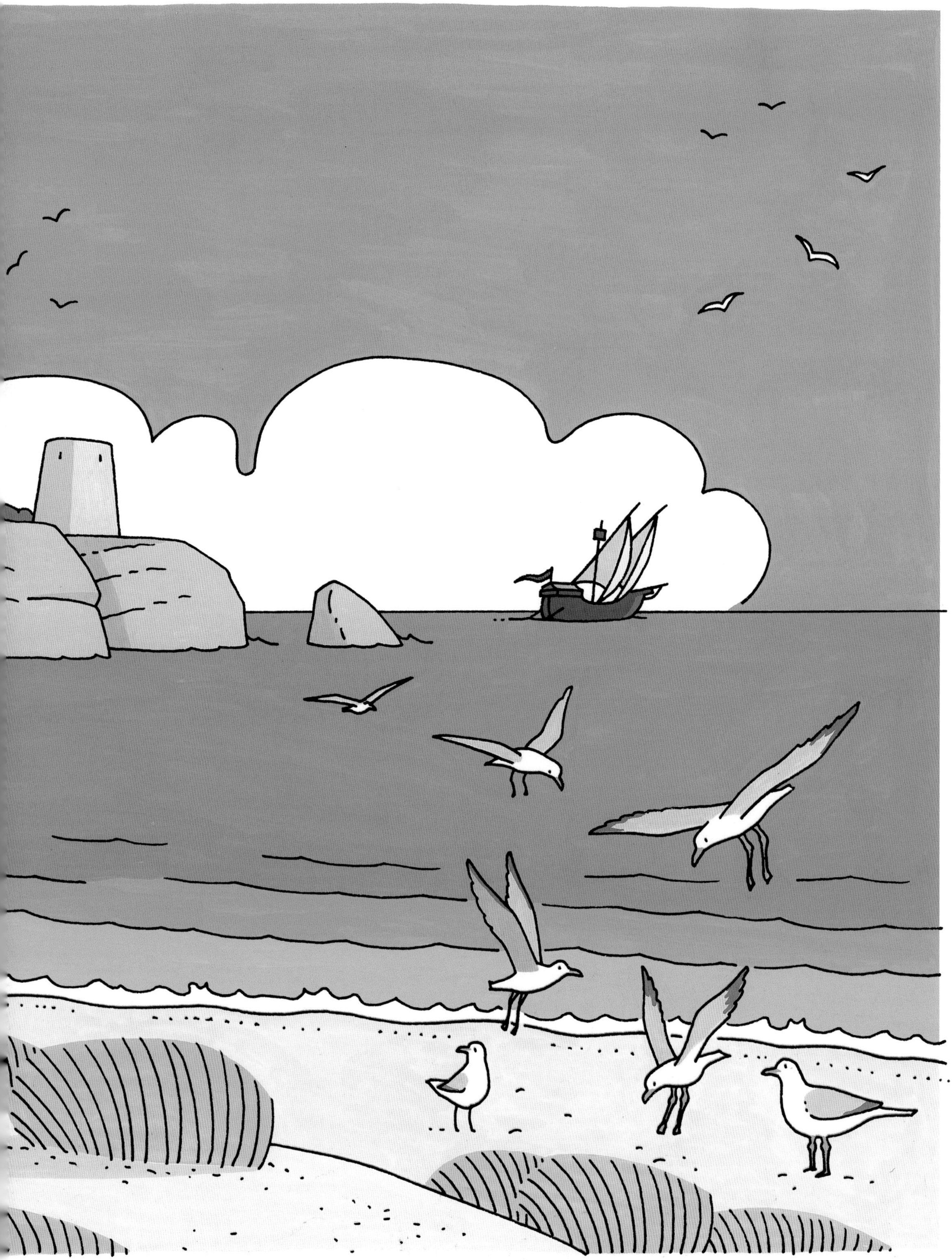

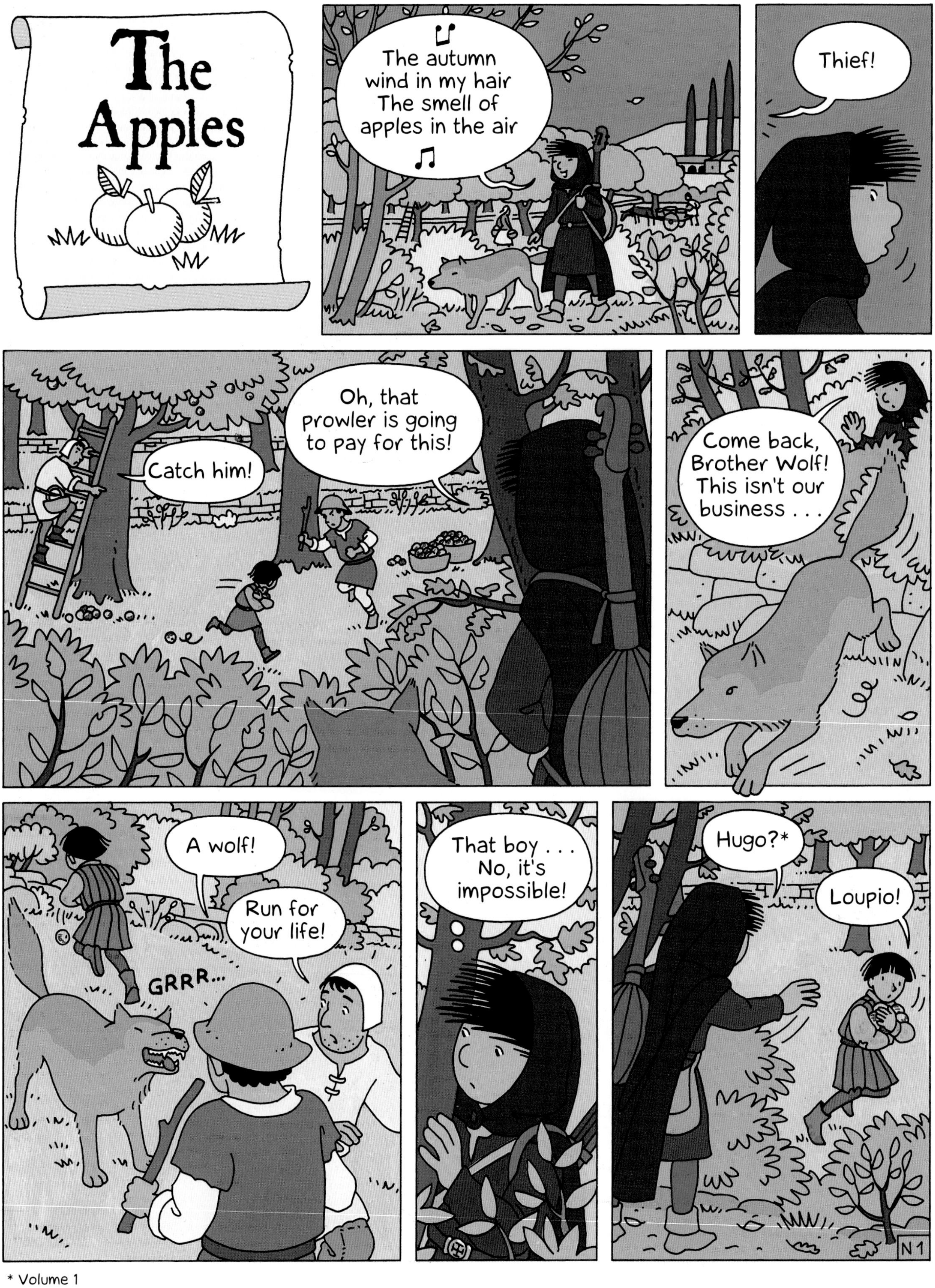
The Apples
The autumn wind in my hair The smell of apples in the air
Thief!
Catch him!
Oh, that prowler is going to pay for this!
Come back, Brother Wolf! This isn't our business . . .
A wolf!
Run for your life!
GRRR...
That boy . . . No, it's impossible!
Hugo?*
Loupio!
N1

* Volume 1

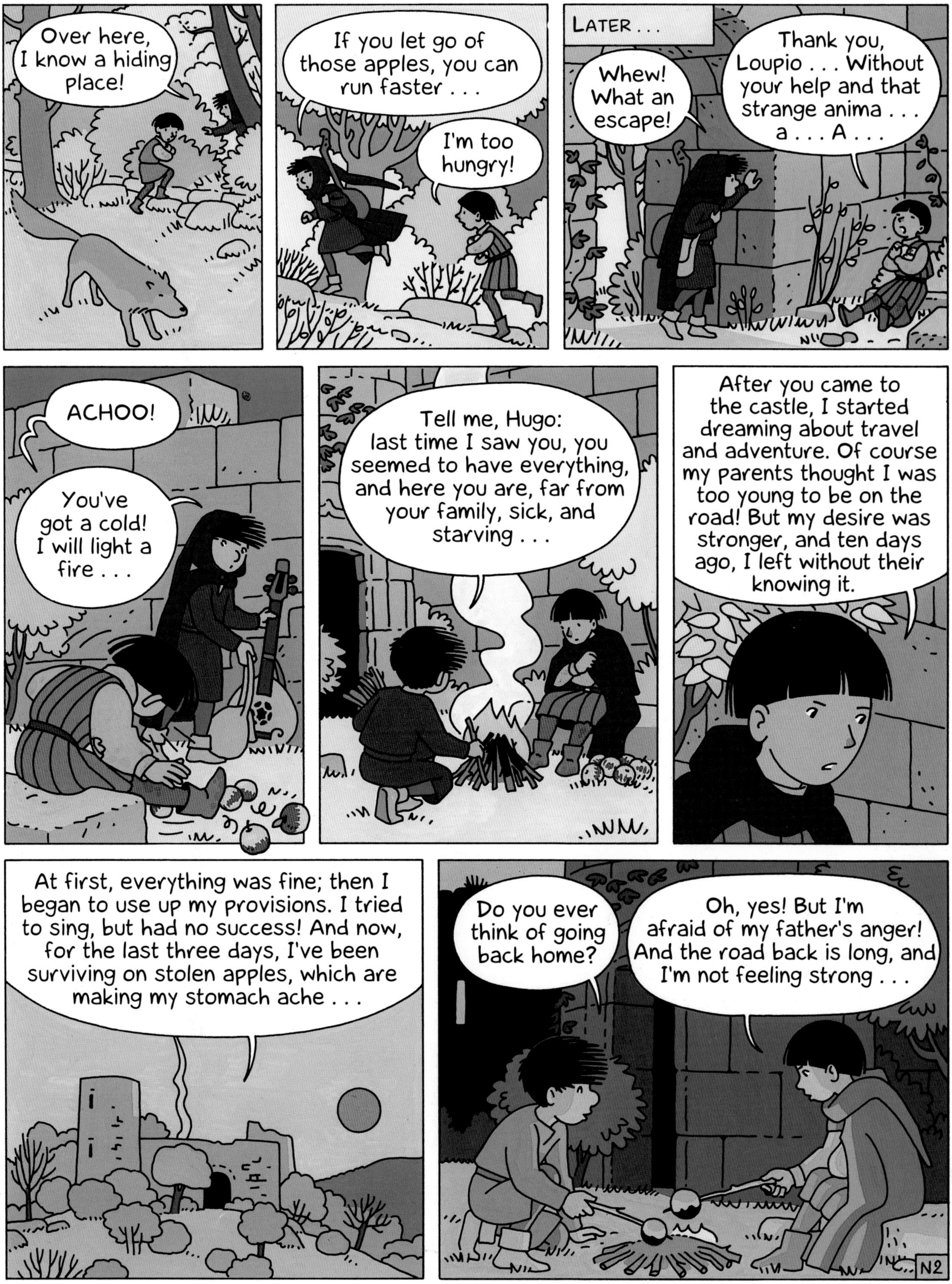
Over here, I know a hiding place!
If you let go of those apples, you can run faster . . .
I'm too hungry!
LATER . . .
Whew! What an escape!
Thank you, Loupio . . . Without your help and that strange anima . . . a . . . A . . .
ACHOO!
You've got a cold! I will light a fire . . .
Tell me, Hugo: last time I saw you, you seemed to have everything, and here you are, far from your family, sick, and starving . . .
After you came to the castle, I started dreaming about travel and adventure. Of course my parents thought I was too young to be on the road! But my desire was stronger, and ten days ago, I left without their knowing it.
At first, everything was fine; then I began to use up my provisions. I tried to sing, but had no success! And now, for the last three days, I've been surviving on stolen apples, which are making my stomach ache . . .
Do you ever think of going back home?
Oh, yes! But I'm afraid of my father's anger! And the road back is long, and I'm not feeling strong . . .
N2

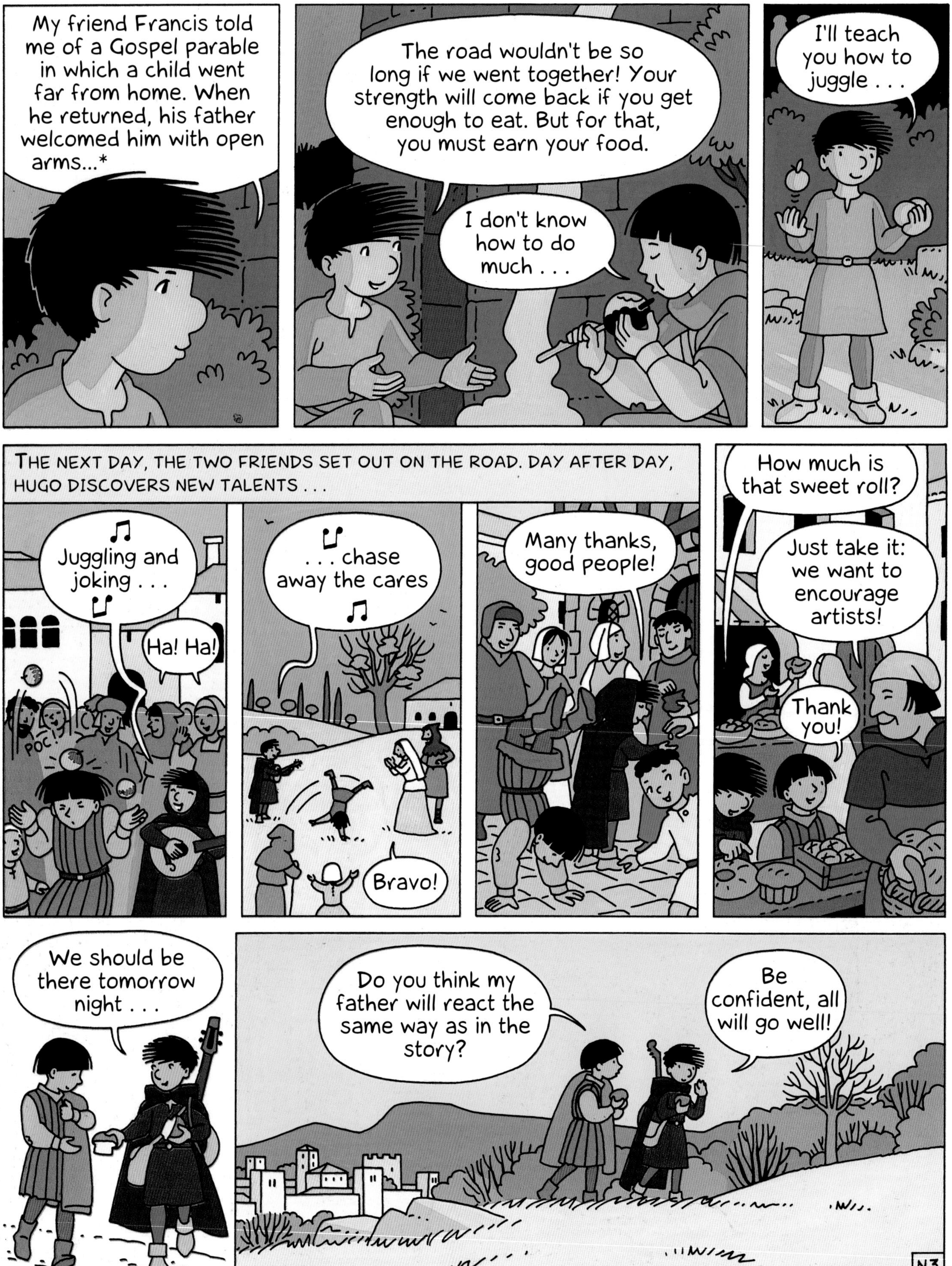
My friend Francis told me of a Gospel parable in which a child went far from home. When he returned, his father welcomed him with open arms...*
The road wouldn't be so long if we went together! Your strength will come back if you get enough to eat. But for that, you must earn your food.
I don't know how to do much . . .
I'll teach you how to juggle . . .
THE NEXT DAY, THE TWO FRIENDS SET OUT ON THE ROAD. DAY AFTER DAY, HUGO DISCOVERS NEW TALENTS . . .
Juggling and joking . . .
Ha! Ha!
POC!
. . . chase away the cares
Bravo!
Many thanks, good people!
How much is that sweet roll?
Just take it: we want to encourage artists!
Thank you!
We should be there tomorrow night . . .
Do you think my father will react the same way as in the story?
Be confident, all will go well!
N3

* Gospel according to Luke, chapter 15, verse 11

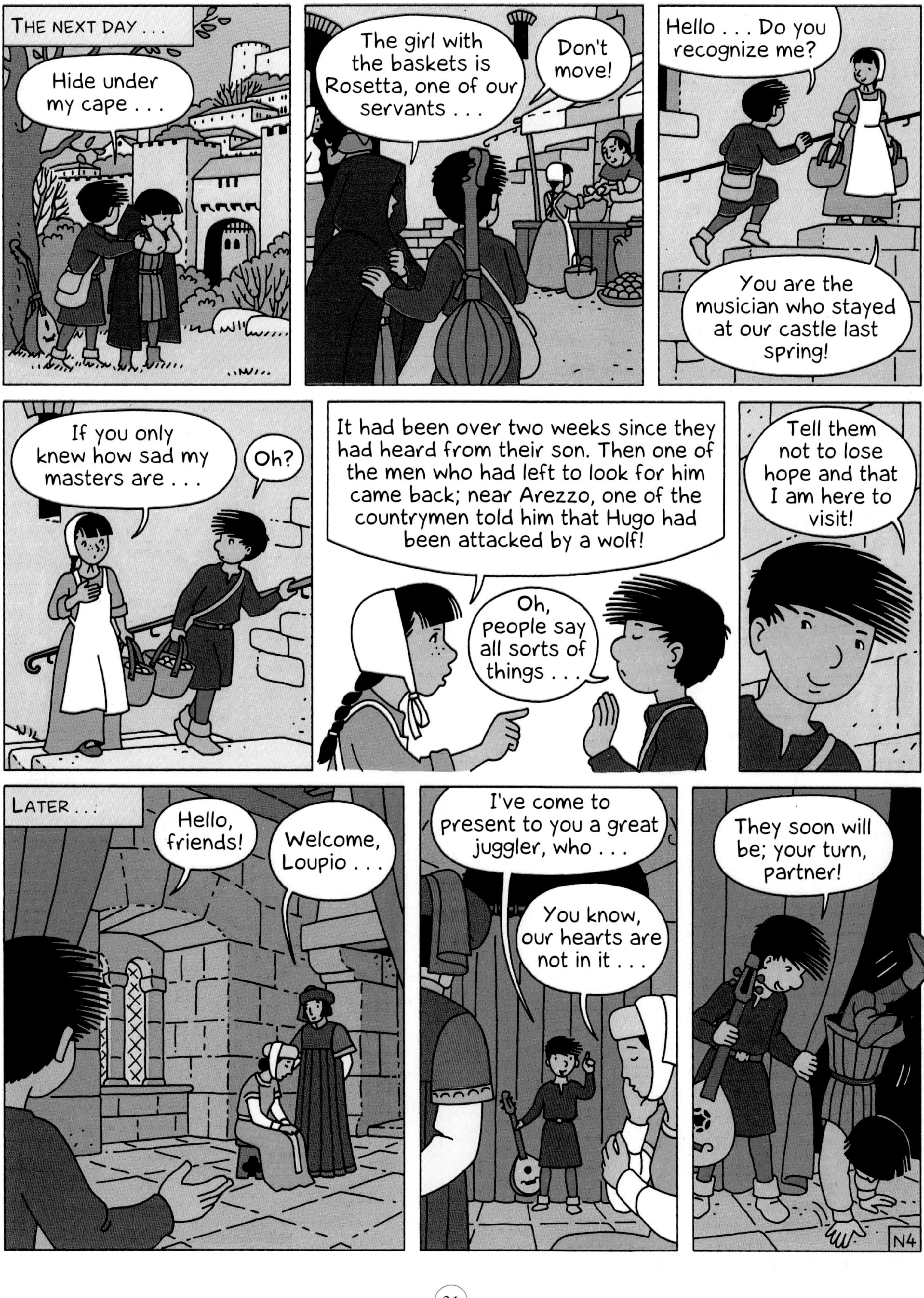
The next day . . .
Hide under my cape . . .
The girl with the baskets is Rosetta, one of our servants . . .
Don't move!
Hello . . . Do you recognize me?
You are the musician who stayed at our castle last spring!
If you only knew how sad my masters are . . .
Oh?
It had been over two weeks since they had heard from their son. Then one of the men who had left to look for him came back; near Arezzo, one of the countrymen told him that Hugo had been attacked by a wolf!
Oh, people say all sorts of things . . .
Tell them not to lose hope and that I am here to visit!
Later . . .
Hello, friends!
Welcome, Loupio . . .
I've come to present to you a great juggler, who . . .
You know, our hearts are not in it . . .
They soon will be; your turn, partner!
N4

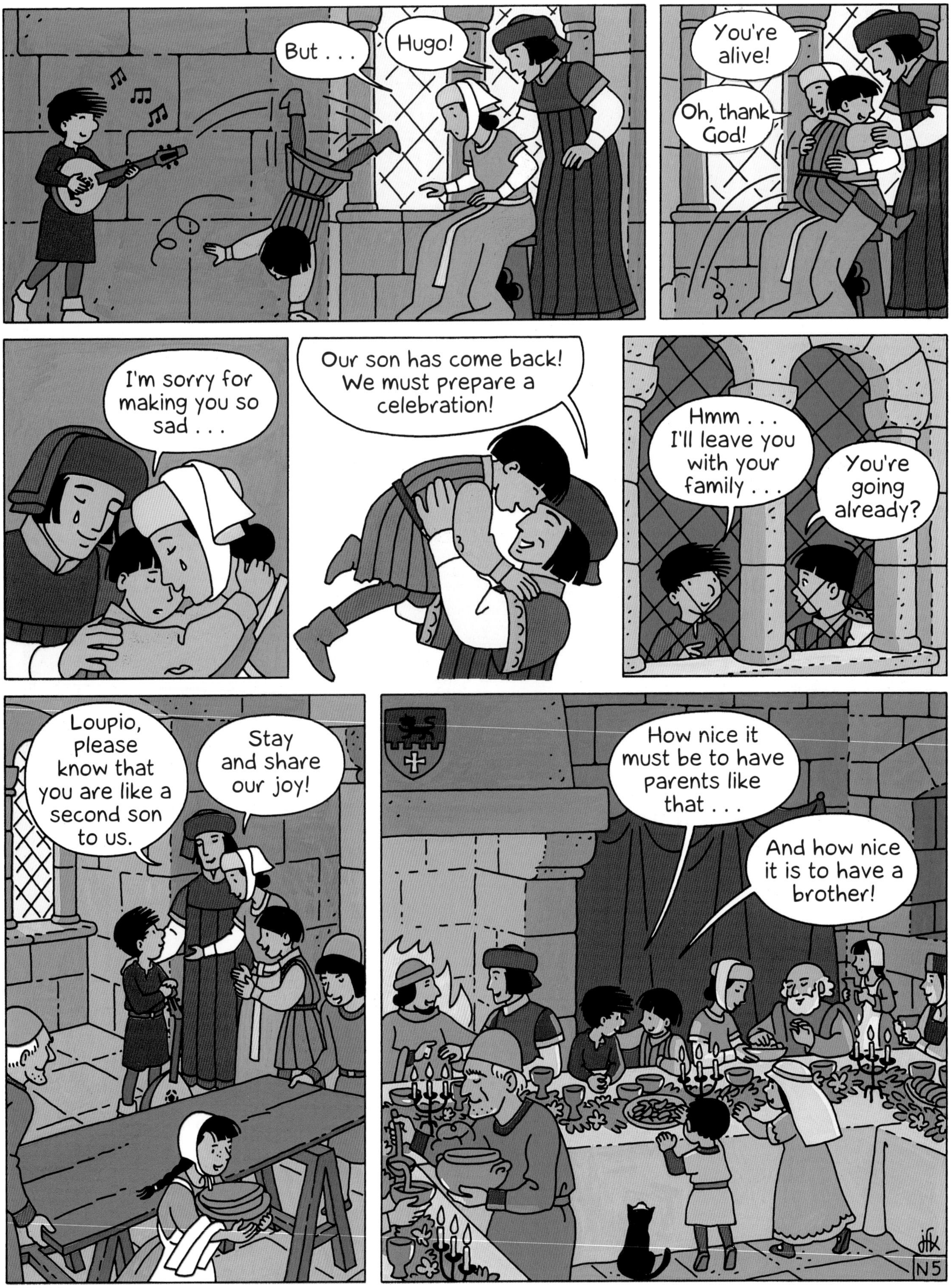
But . . .
Hugo!
You're alive!
Oh, thank God!
I'm sorry for making you so sad . . .
Our son has come back! We must prepare a celebration!
Hmm . . . I'll leave you with your family . . .
You're going already?
Loupio, please know that you are like a second son to us.
Stay and share our joy!
How nice it must be to have parents like that . . .
And how nice it is to have a brother!
N5

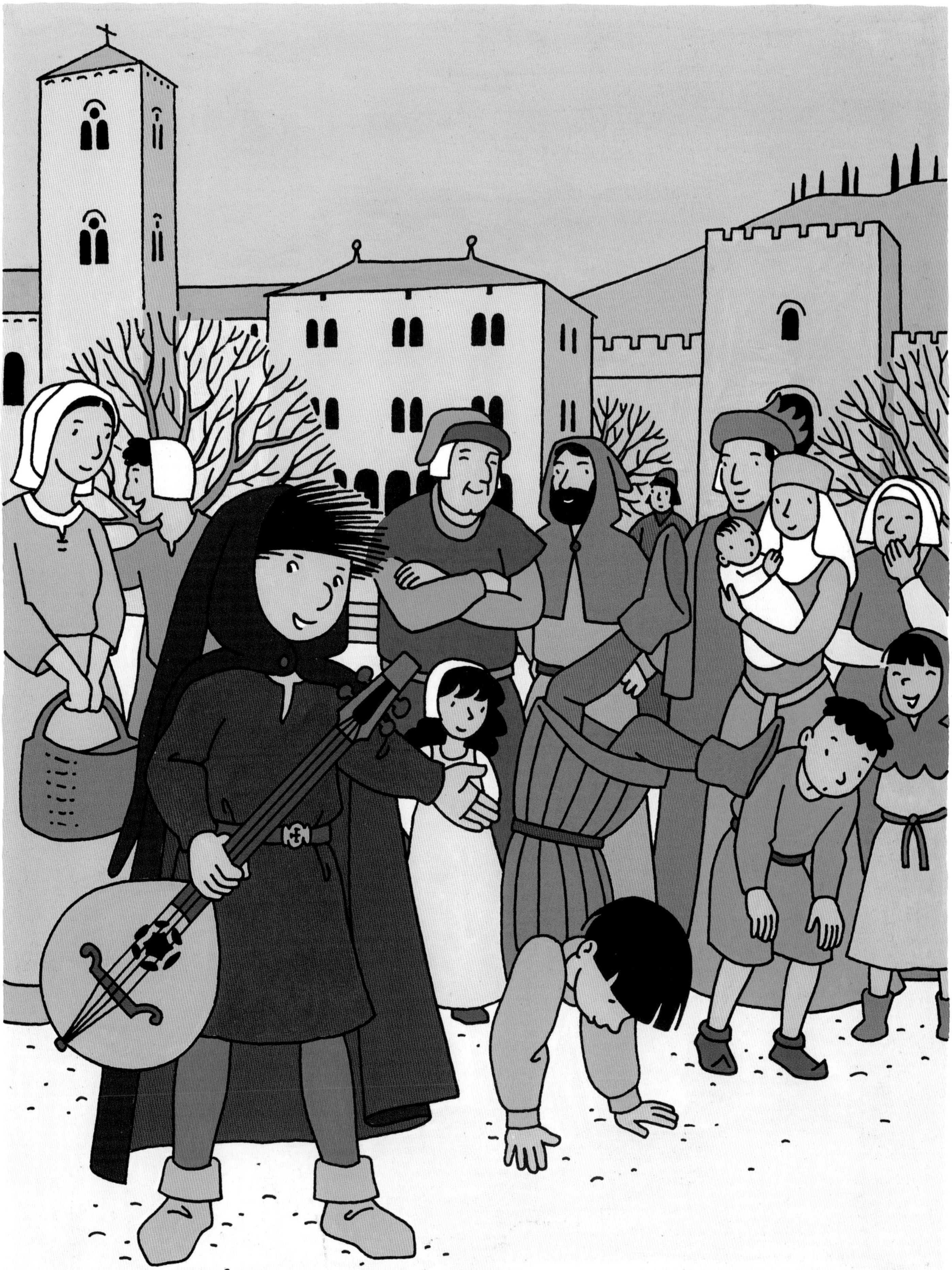

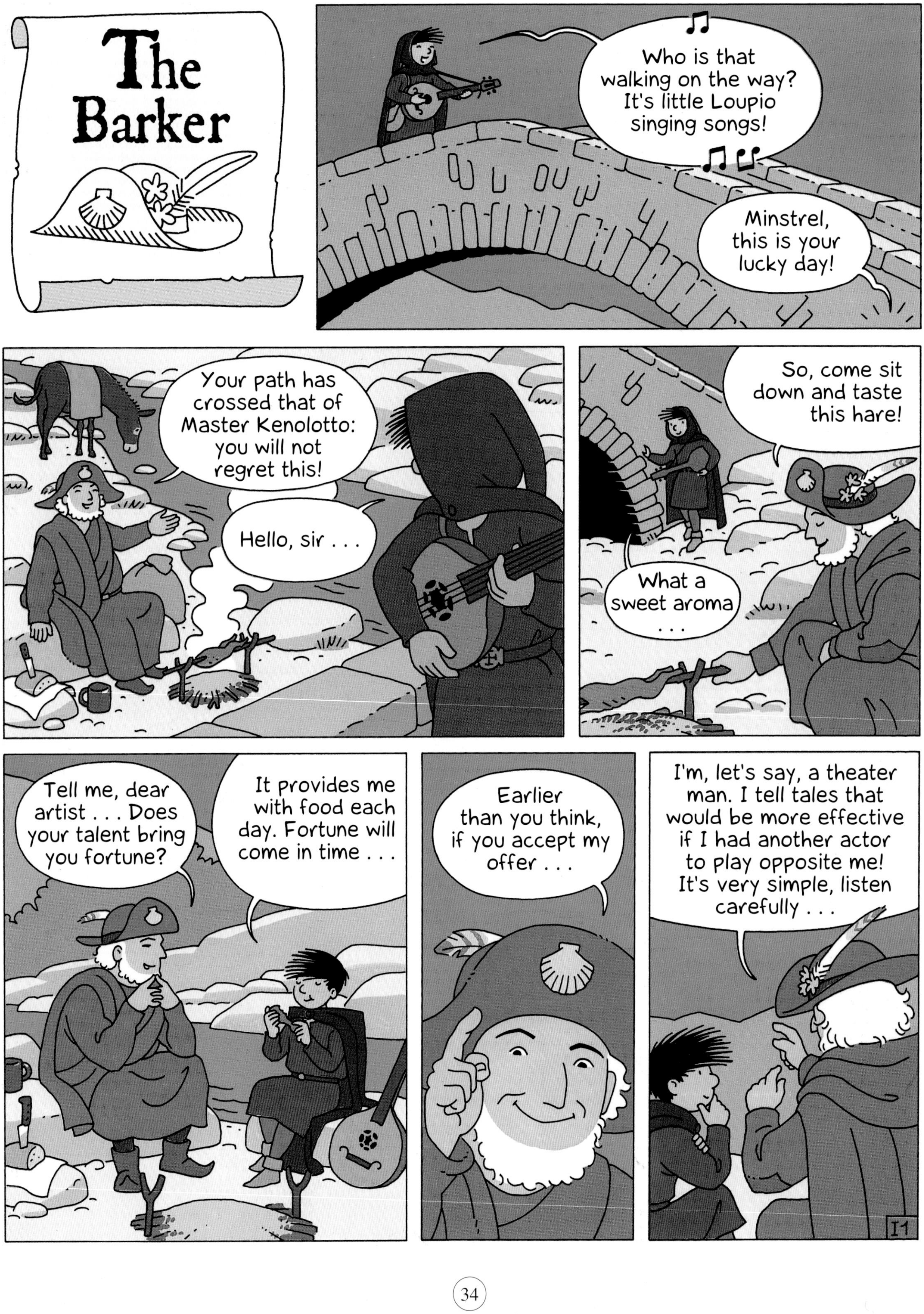
The Barker
Who is that walking on the way? It's little Loupio singing songs!
Minstrel, this is your lucky day!
Your path has crossed that of Master Kenolotto: you will not regret this!
Hello, sir . . .
So, come sit down and taste this hare!
What a sweet aroma . . .
Tell me, dear artist . . . Does your talent bring you fortune?
It provides me with food each day. Fortune will come in time . . .
Earlier than you think, if you accept my offer . . .
I'm, let's say, a theater man. I tell tales that would be more effective if I had another actor to play opposite me! It's very simple, listen carefully . . .
I1

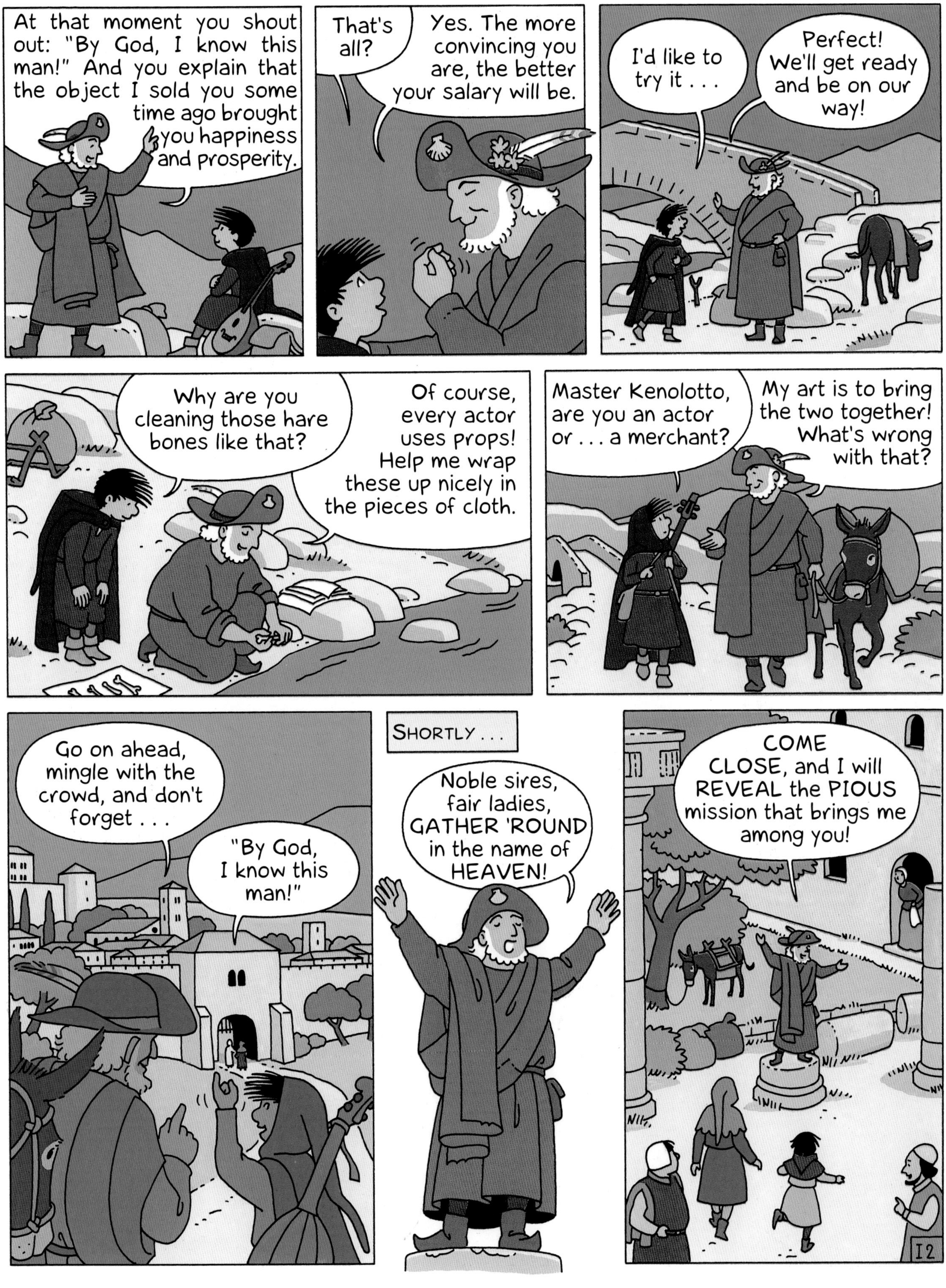
At that moment you shout out: "By God, I know this man!" And you explain that the object I sold you some time ago brought you happiness and prosperity.
That's all?
Yes. The more convincing you are, the better your salary will be.
I'd like to try it . . .
Perfect! We'll get ready and be on our way!
Why are you cleaning those hare bones like that?
Of course, every actor uses props! Help me wrap these up nicely in the pieces of cloth.
Master Kenolotto, are you an actor or . . . a merchant?
My art is to bring the two together! What's wrong with that?
Go on ahead, mingle with the crowd, and don't forget . . .
"By God, I know this man!"
SHORTLY . . .
Noble sires, fair ladies, GATHER 'ROUND in the name of HEAVEN!
COME CLOSE, and I will REVEAL the PIOUS mission that brings me among you!
I2

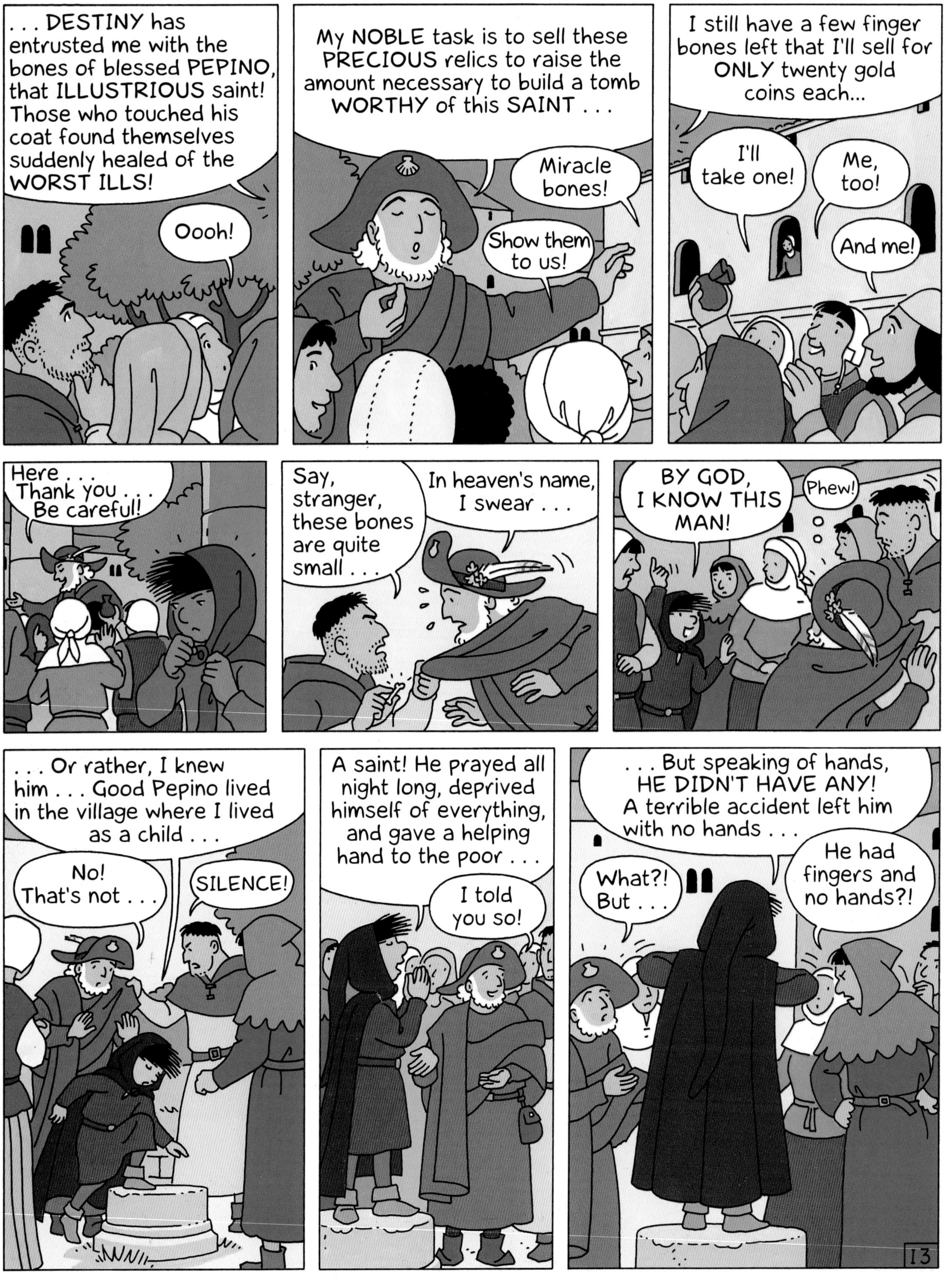
. . . DESTINY has entrusted me with the bones of blessed PEPINO, that ILLUSTRIOUS saint! Those who touched his coat found themselves suddenly healed of the WORST ILLS!
Oooh!
My NOBLE task is to sell these PRECIOUS relics to raise the amount necessary to build a tomb WORTHY of this SAINT . . .
Miracle bones!
Show them to us!
I still have a few finger bones left that I'll sell for ONLY twenty gold coins each...
I'll take one!
Me, too!
And me!
Here . . . Thank you . . . Be careful!
Say, stranger, these bones are quite small . . .
In heaven's name, I swear . . .
BY GOD, I KNOW THIS MAN!
Phew!
. . . Or rather, I knew him . . . Good Pepino lived in the village where I lived as a child . . .
No! That's not . . .
SILENCE!
A saint! He prayed all night long, deprived himself of everything, and gave a helping hand to the poor . . .
I told you so!
. . . But speaking of hands, HE DIDN'T HAVE ANY! A terrible accident left him with no hands . . .
What?! But . . .
He had fingers and no hands?!
13

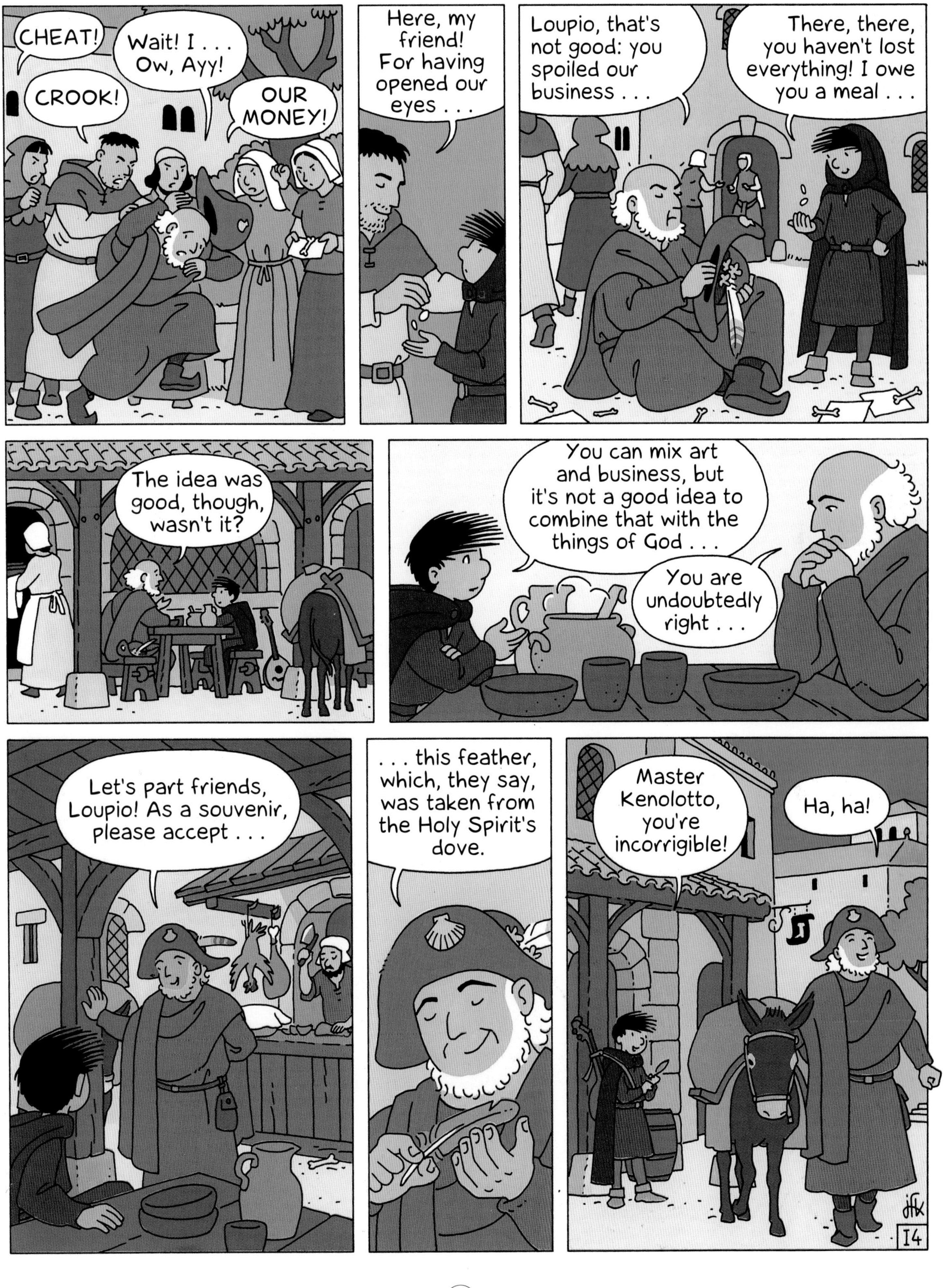
CHEAT!
Wait! I . . . Ow, Ayy!
CROOK!
OUR MONEY!
Here, my friend! For having opened our eyes . . .
Loupio, that's not good: you spoiled our business . . .
There, there, you haven't lost everything! I owe you a meal . . .
The idea was good, though, wasn't it?
You can mix art and business, but it's not a good idea to combine that with the things of God . . .
You are undoubtedly right . . .
Let's part friends, Loupio! As a souvenir, please accept . . .
. . . this feather, which, they say, was taken from the Holy Spirit's dove.
Master Kenolotto, you're incorrigible!
Ha, ha!
I4

The Dogs

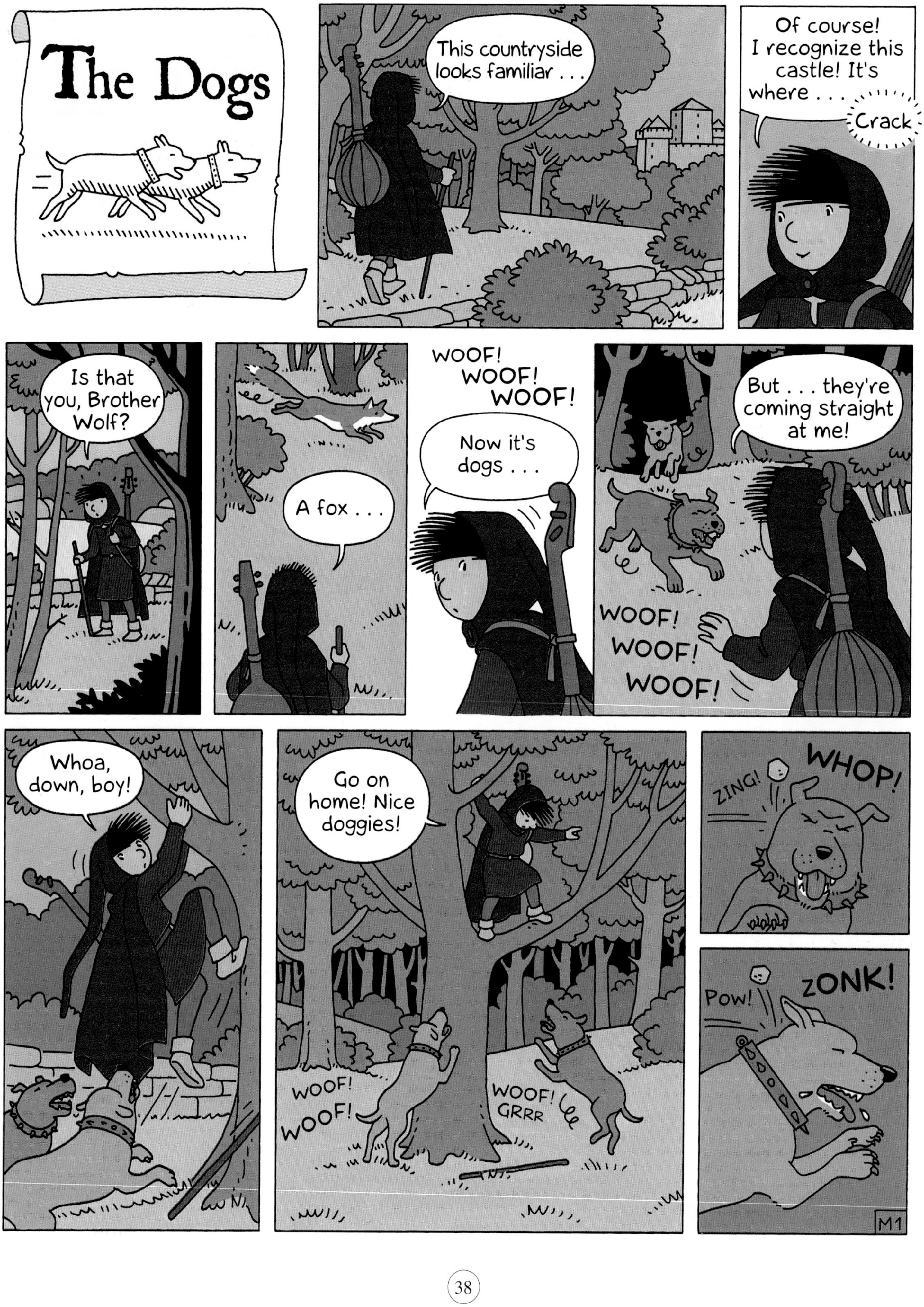
This countryside looks familiar . . .
Of course! I recognize this castle! It's where . . .
Crack
Is that you, Brother Wolf?
A fox . . .
WOOF! WOOF! WOOF!
Now it's dogs . . .
But . . . they're coming straight at me!
WOOF! WOOF! WOOF!
Whoa, down, boy!
Go on home! Nice doggies!
WOOF! WOOF!
WOOF! GRRR
ZING!
WHOP!
POW!
ZONK!
M1

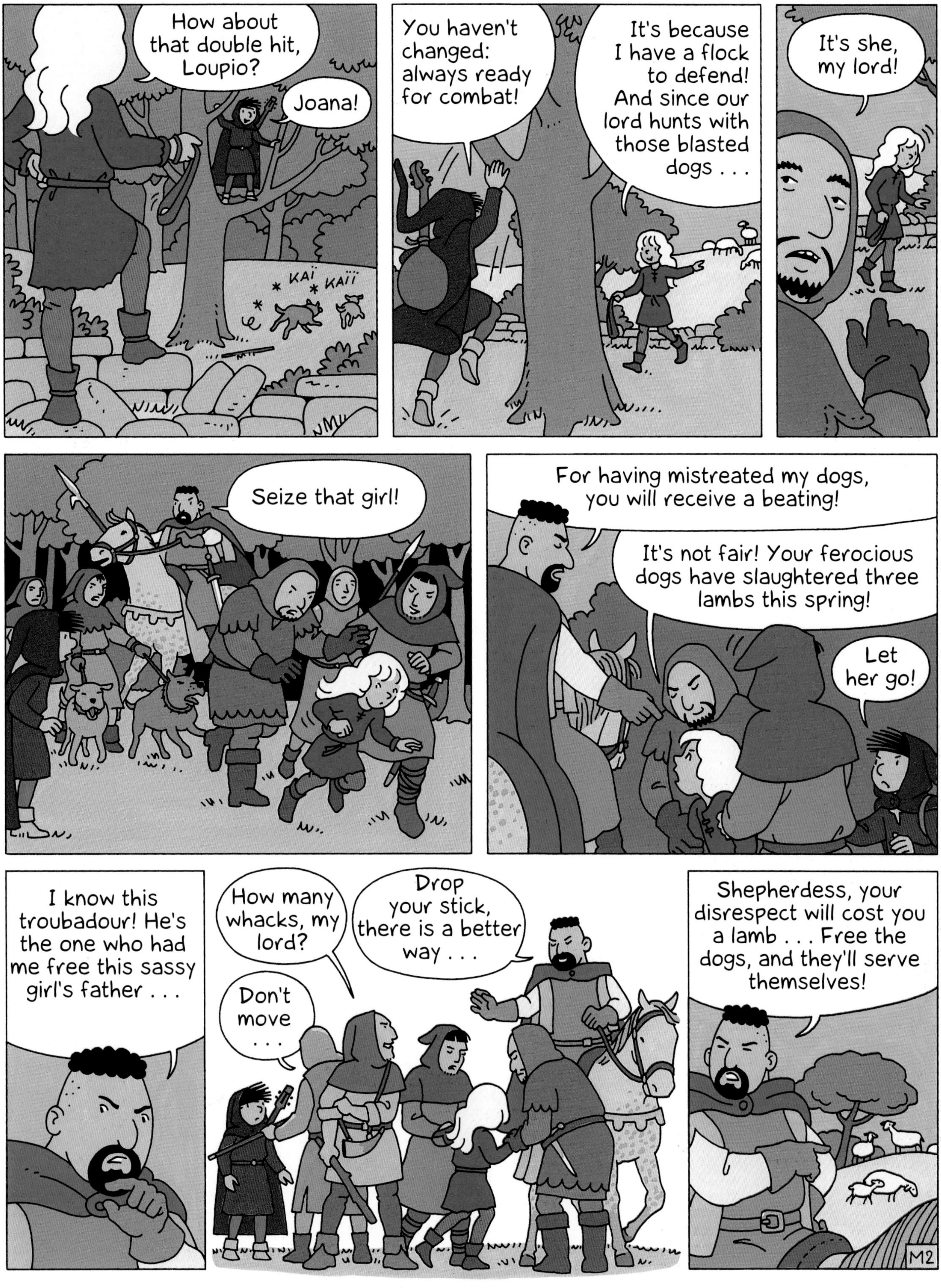
How about that double hit, Loupio?
Joana!
KAÏ
KAÏÏ
You haven't changed: always ready for combat!
It's because I have a flock to defend! And since our lord hunts with those blasted dogs . . .
It's she, my lord!
Seize that girl!
For having mistreated my dogs, you will receive a beating!
It's not fair! Your ferocious dogs have slaughtered three lambs this spring!
Let her go!
I know this troubadour! He's the one who had me free this sassy girl's father . . .
How many whacks, my lord?
Drop your stick, there is a better way . . .
Don't move . . .
Shepherdess, your disrespect will cost you a lamb . . . Free the dogs, and they'll serve themselves!
M2

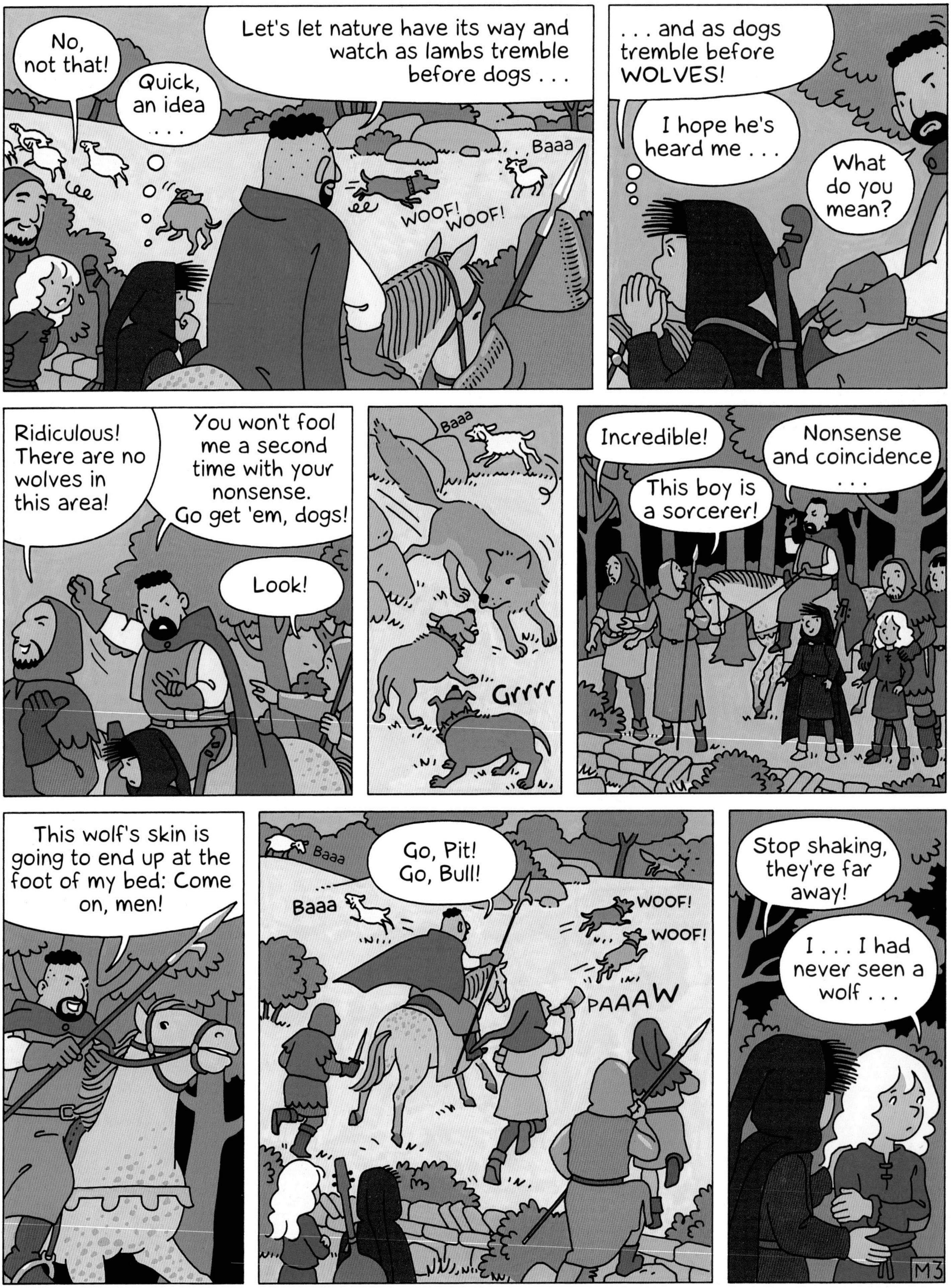
No, not that!
Quick, an idea . . .
Let's let nature have its way and watch as lambs tremble before dogs . . .
Baaa
WOOF! WOOF!
. . . and as dogs tremble before WOLVES!
I hope he's heard me . . .
What do you mean?
Ridiculous! There are no wolves in this area!
You won't fool me a second time with your nonsense. Go get 'em, dogs!
Look!
Baaa
Grrrr
Incredible!
This boy is a sorcerer!
Nonsense and coincidence . . .
This wolf's skin is going to end up at the foot of my bed: Come on, men!
Baaa
Go, Pit! Go, Bull!
Baaa
WOOF!
WOOF!
PAAAW
Stop shaking, they're far away!
I . . . I had never seen a wolf . . .
M3

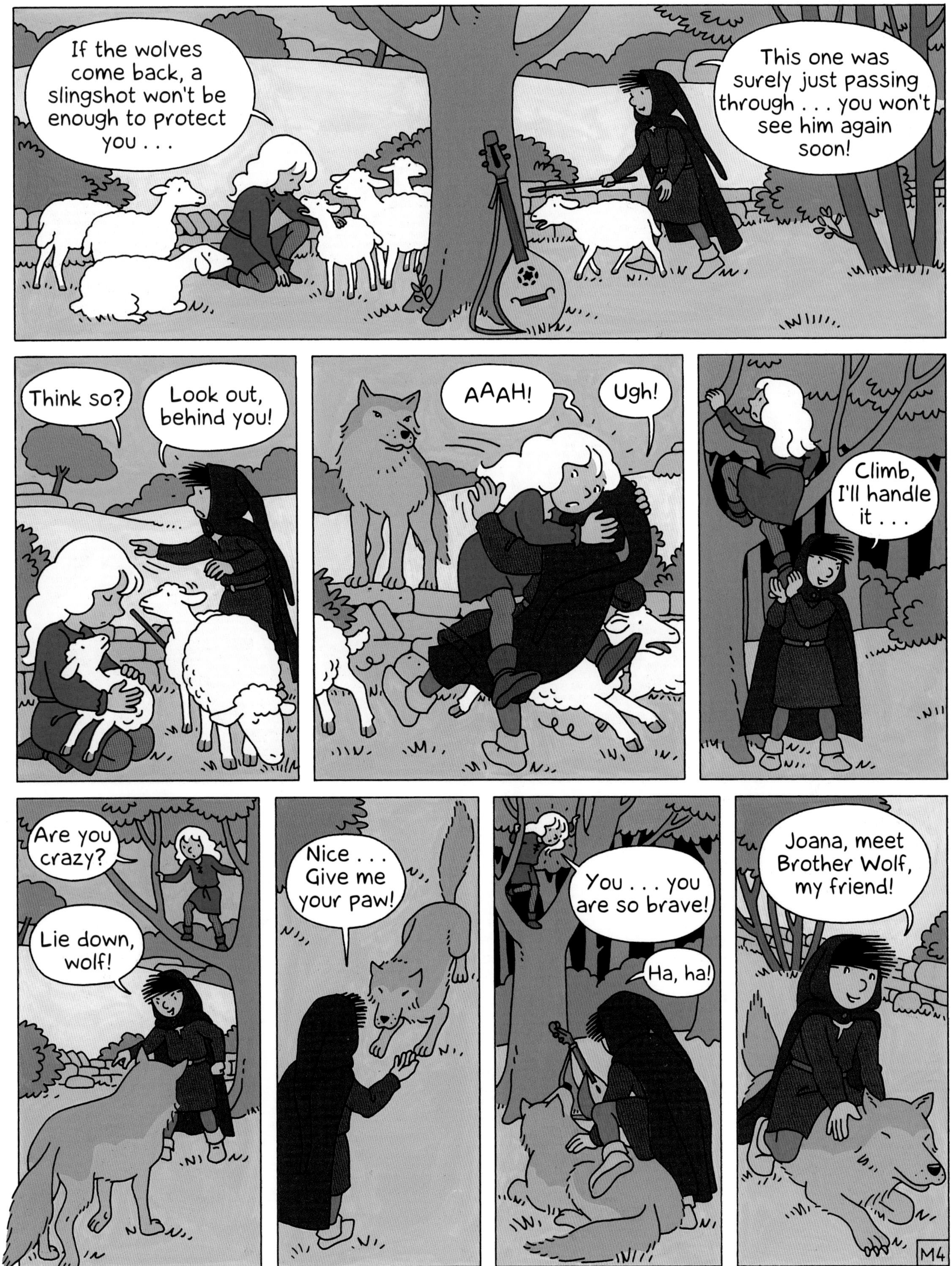
If the wolves come back, a slingshot won't be enough to protect you . . .
This one was surely just passing through . . . you won't see him again soon!
Think so?
Look out, behind you!
AAAH!
Ugh!
Climb, I'll handle it . . .
Are you crazy?
Lie down, wolf!
Nice . . . Give me your paw!
You . . . you are so brave!
Ha, ha!
Joana, meet Brother Wolf, my friend!
M4

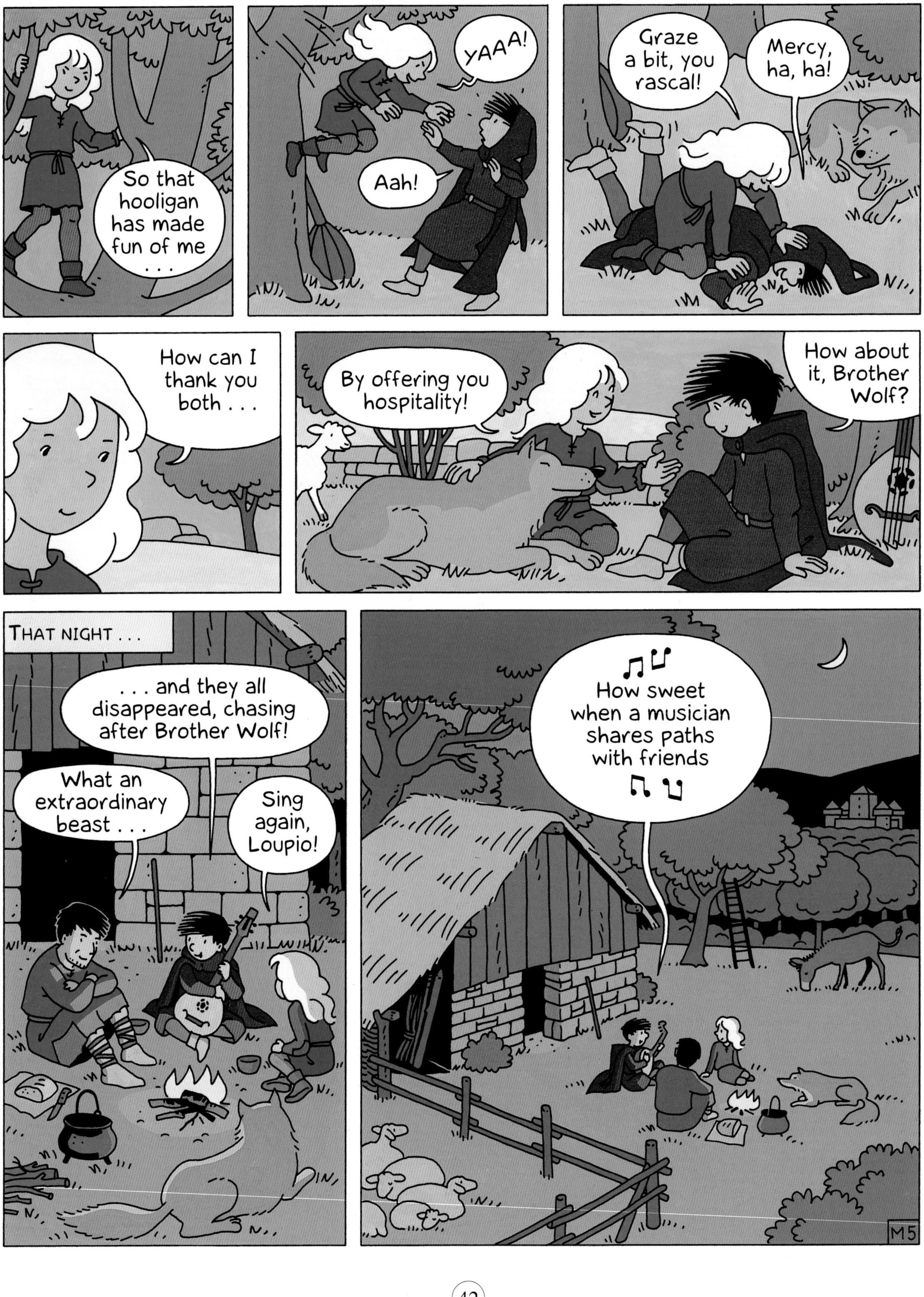
So that hooligan has made fun of me . . .
YAAA!
Aah!
Graze a bit, you rascal!
Mercy, ha, ha!
How can I thank you both . . .
By offering you hospitality!
How about it, Brother Wolf?
THAT NIGHT . . .
. . . and they all disappeared, chasing after Brother Wolf!
What an extraordinary beast . . .
Sing again, Loupio!
How sweet when a musician shares paths with friends
M5

The March of the Minstrel

REFRAIN: Solo, then all

As I tra - vel on the roads, I'll be sing-ing my songs.

I'm a mins-trel on the march! What a beau-ti-ful life!

VERSES: Solo

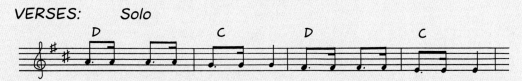

When I'm march-ing on my way, sing - ing through a - noth-er day,

Solo, then all

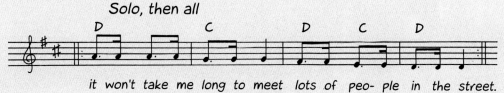

it won't take me long to meet lots of peo- ple in the street.

Refrain: As I travel on the roads,
I'll be singing my songs.
I'm a minstrel on the march!
What a beautiful life! (repeat)

When I'm marching on my way,
singing through another day,
it won't take me long to meet
lots of people in the street. (repeat)

Brave Joana's great delight
would be to become a knight.
I wouldn't have known her, though,
had I only stayed at home. (repeat)

Hunters, each with knife and bow,
fishermen, I've come to know.
Had we never shouted "Hi!"
we'd be strangers passing by. (repeat)

Hugo travels by my side
through the country far and wide.
We would not be friends right now
if we hadn't met somehow. (repeat)

Kenolotto won't prevail
with the fakes he has for sale.
If I'd never come along,
he would not be in this song! (repeat)

If you're lonely, bored, or blue,
go outside to some place new.
Here is what I recommend:
March and sing and find a friend! (repeat)

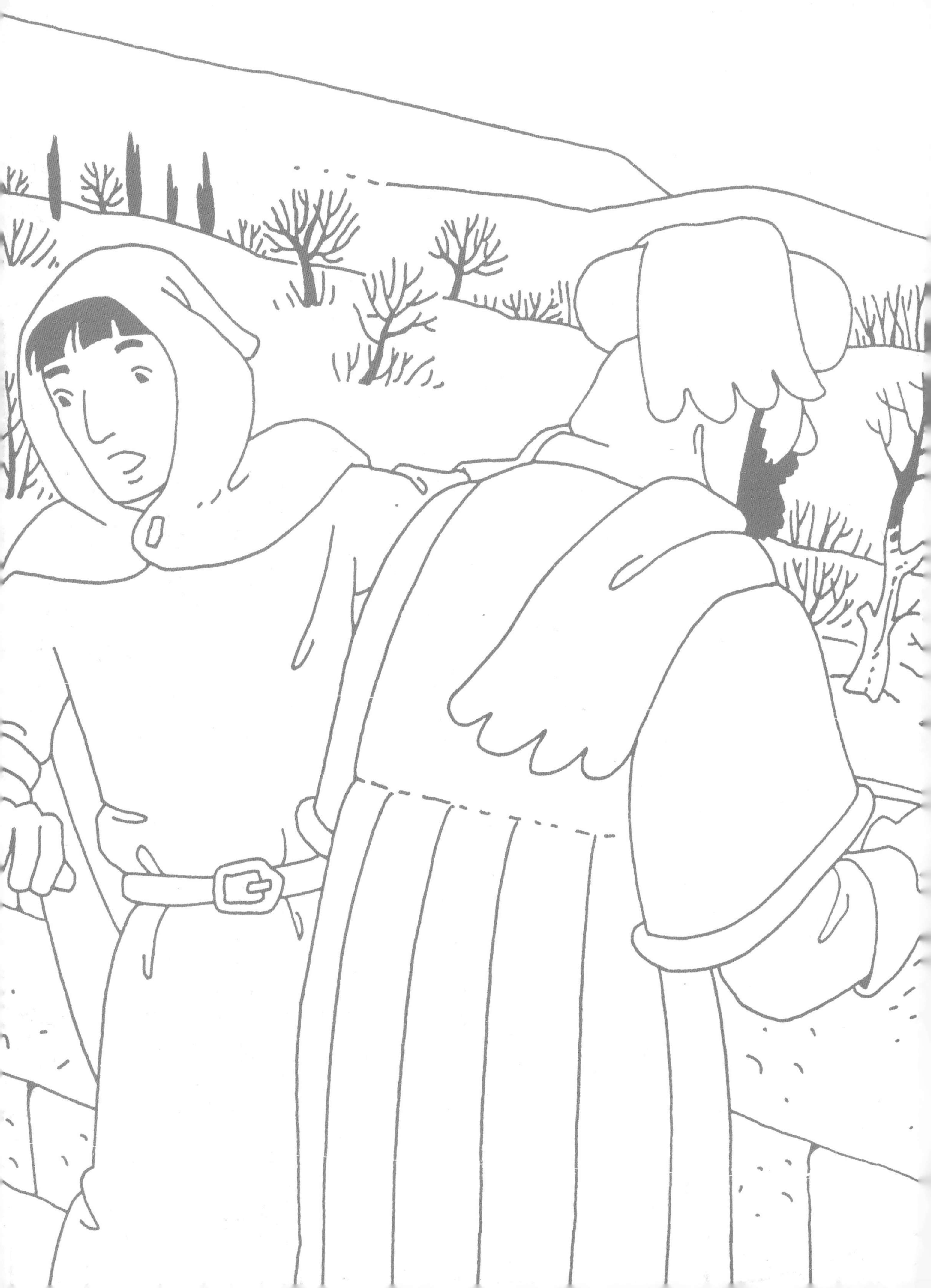